ORDIN*

BOY

Life was about to become

anything but ordinary

By

Richard Bradley

Copyright © Richard Bradley 2024
This book is sold subject to the condition that it shall not, by way of trade or otherwise, be lent, resold, hired out, or otherwise circulated without the publisher's prior consent in any form of binding or cover other than that in which it is published and without a similar condition including this condition being imposed on the subsequent publisher.
The moral right of Richard Bradley has been asserted.
ISBN: 9798335910798

This is a work of fiction. Names, characters, businesses, places, events and incidents are either the products of the author's imagination or used in a fictitious manner. Any resemblance to actual persons, living or dead, or actual events is purely coincidental.

To Glyn, who encouraged me to take the first step.

CONTENTS

- CHAPTER 1 1
- CHAPTER 2 14
- CHAPTER 3 29
- CHAPTER 4 41
- CHAPTER 5 54
- CHAPTER 6 66
- CHAPTER 7 78
- CHAPTER 8 87
- CHAPTER 9 97
- CHAPTER 10 114
- CHAPTER 11 137
- CHAPTER 12 161
- CHAPTER 13 164
- CHAPTER 14 173
- CHAPTER 15 179
- CHAPTER 16 204
- CHAPTER 17 210
- CHAPTER 18 216
- CHAPTER 19 241
- CHAPTER 20 258
- CHAPTER 21 260

My name is Daniel Ross… but everyone calls me Danny!

I am sixteen, going on seventeen.

I live with my dad; he's my best friend.

My mum died when I was fourteen and I still get emotional every time she's mentioned.

Oh yes, and I have a thing for Doc Martens. Well, no, it's not a thing. I'm making it sound a bit, you know, well, maybe I do have a thing?

I'm blushing right now. Good job you can't see!

I'm just an ordinary boy and this is the ordinary story of my ordinary life, one ordinary first term in sixth form.

I am making absolutely no excuse for this being a gentle love story with a little bit of turbulence along the way. We need a bit of love in 2024. Actually, we all need a lot of love, it would certainly make the world a better place to live in.

Maybe I'll call my story…

ORDINARY BOY

Oh, crikey, that makes me sound very boring. Maybe you won't want to read about me. Maybe I'll big it up a bit.

OK, I'm thinking!

This is harder than you can imagine!

What's that, you say? Go back to the Doc Martens bit; that sounded interesting? Trust me, it's not!

I'm blushing again.

I'm also realising I'm using too many exclamation marks. Perhaps I have a fetish for punctuation?

It all started on…

CHAPTER 1
Friday 15th September

I look at Dad and screw my face up just a little bit.

"What?" he asks.

"Are you really wearing that shirt?" I question his choice.

"What's wrong with it?"

"If you have to ask…" I pause, feeling guilty that I am about to ruin his first date since Mum died.

It was Katie who had suggested it. Katie is my bestest friend in the world, well, after Dad, coz we just are.

Katie had come round one night a few weeks ago and we were surfing – no, not on the beach, but as my gramps would have said, on the wonderweb.

"There's a site here called Sum Body 4 U," she said, twirling a strand of hair.

"Somebody for you?" I enquired. "What's that about?"

"It's a dating thing. A play on words, I suppose," she added vaguely.

"I don't get it," I said, feeling very confused. It had been a long first day in sixth form, all a bit strange.

"It's a site for people who like figures."

I looked at her blankly.

"Accountants. Like your dad."

I carried on looking at her, slightly bemused, so she swung her laptop around.

"Oh," I exclaimed, the penny dropping. "Sum as in, well, sums. Yes, it's a play on words. I didn't get it."

"Obvs not."

Sometimes you have to think outside the box with Katie. This was one of those moments.

"So," I said, trying to work out where this was heading, "you think we should get Dad a girlfriend?"

"Would that be such a bad thing? If you're off to uni eventually, he's going to be on his own." Katie took a deep breath. "Maybe it's time?" She looked at me, a tiny bit scared.

I tried to hold back a tear that was forming. "You're right," I gulped.

I could NOT imagine anyone else with my dad and maybe that was selfish. He had every right to be happy.

Who knows? One day I might be happy with someone.

"If you think it's a bad idea…" Katie started.

"No, you're right. You do realise that he maybe doesn't want a girlfriend," I suggested. "He hasn't really shown any interest and certainly never mentioned it."

"Maybe he's worried how you would feel?" Katie continued. "Maybe if you suggested it? Or is that too weird?"

"Probably, but it could be the only way."

So, that is how we come to where we are on this Friday evening. I think it was four weeks ago we signed Dad up on the Sum Body 4 U website. I have grown to hate the name of the website, but that's by the by.

"So, not this shirt?" Dad asks.

I sort of try not to pull a face at his choice. After all, he has to be comfortable.

But his choice is bloody awful.

My phone pings.

I look in his wardrobe and bring out a plain, pale blue shirt with a Charles Tyrwhitt label. Dad has good taste but I think he is trying too hard today.

"Perhaps just keep it plain and simple," I suggest. He's put on a pair of tan chinos and the blue will work really well with them.

"I'm actually taking fashion advice from my son." He smiles. "But, yes, you're right. I'll maybe keep the stripey one for if I get to know her better."

Or maybe just put it in the charity bag, I think to myself.

My phone pings again.

Dad's date is Evie. She is thirty-nine, separated from her husband, works in finance at a supermarket chain, lives in a flat in town. Long blonde hair, nice smile, likes dogs, GSOH.

Oh my! An accountant with a sense of humour. Actually, Dad is an accountant. Could I live with two accountants, both with GSOH, a Labrador, and her collection of vintage clothing? Is this a good idea?

Dad seems OK with the prospect. It is time and as Katie had suggested, the idea needed to come from me.

My phone pings for the third time.

"Do you need to get those?" Dad asks.

"It will be Katie, she wants pictures."

"What of?"

"You."

"Seriously?"

"Yep."

"Go on then." Dad pulls his shirt out. I pull a face. "In or out?" he adds.

"Always in, Dad, it's not 1997."

"What should I do with my hair?" he asks, ruffling it up a bit.

"Just what you always do, Dad."

He smooths it down and heads into the ensuite.

My phone pings yet again.

I open it up. Sure enough, they are all from Katie.

What trousers did he go for?

Have you chosen his shirt?

What about his hair?

I reply:

All good, he looks stunning.

A shocked face emoji is sent in return.

Dad is back in the room; he takes a deep breath in.

"OK?" I ask.

"Bit scared, if I'm honest."

"Bound to be. It's been a while."

Then, it goes quiet. We both know we are thinking about Mum. She would be so cool with this, though. She would have chosen the blue shirt. Thanks for giving me good taste, Mum. She might have gone for a different belt but the one Dad has chosen is fine. I don't want to make him any more paranoid than he already is.

He looks at his watch.

"What time are you meeting up?" I ask.

"Seven. Maybe I'll go, take it easy, not arrive flustered."

"Always a good idea."

I feel like I'm sending my child off to school for the first day as I watch Dad get in the car. I want to rush out and bring him back and tell him everything will be OK. Shouldn't he be a little bit excited? He looks happier going off to the dentist, frankly.

I close the door and lean against it.

Talk about role reversal.

My phone pings.

Has he gone yet?

I pressed WhatsApp audio and Katie connects on the first ring.

"So?" she asks, all rabbit eyed.

"I feel awful. He looked so small."

"What have we done? Will you blame me if it goes wrong?"

"Totally. No question."

Katie sighs and looks downcast. "It was a good idea, could be he's just still not ready."

"Time will tell. Of course, perhaps he just doesn't want anyone else."

"Your mum was brilliant. Hard act to follow."

"Very." Now it's my turn to sigh. "Let's talk about something else."

There's a pause, as if we can't think of anything else to talk about. We have only been friends for like, forever. We can normally talk ourselves hoarse.

Eventually Katie breaks the silence. "What about that new guy?"

"What new guy?" I ask, my interest rising.

"He was in maths."

"I'm not in your set for maths," I point out.

"Yeah, but I thought you would have known."

A Katie moment again. Two in one night! I raise my eyebrows and stare at her. "So, tell me about him."

"You interested?"

"I might be."

Now you're wondering why I might be interested.

Go on, you know you are.

I told you I am gay as well, right?

Come on, I did, back at the start, the bit between the thing about Doc Martens and... Oh yeah, got carried away, must have forgotten.

Oh, well, you know now.

Only, no-one knows apart from Katie and Jordan; you'll find out about Jordan in a bit.

But you said your best friend was your dad. Don't you tell him everything?

Wait, whose book is this? I tell the story; don't ask questions I'm not ready to provide a suitably insane answer to.

No, I haven't told Dad, haven't got a suitably insane answer to that yet. It's all a fairly new thing. Well, not a new thing but only really confirmed to myself and Katie following a quiz she got me to do online called 'How Gay Are You?'

Why? I hear you ask.

Stop with all the questions.

It was a bit of fun. You know the sort of thing. Britney Spears or Pink? Red socks or stripey ones? There was even a question about Doc Martens. I kid you not. Apparently, you're more likely to be gay than not if you wear Doc Martens.

Who would have known?

Well, I do now. Apparently.

Anyway, I digress. Katie is waiting to tell me about the 'new guy.'

I'll come back to the gay quiz later.

Promise!

"So? I ask again, having been rudely interrupted.

"OK, so he's in my maths set."

"Yep."

"He's kinda cute; he's your height and build."

I could feel a 'set-up' coming here. Katie is desperate to get me hooked up, but it's a bit tricky when only your best friends – not my dad, to be clear – knows about how gay you are; 87% according to the gay quiz, for your information.

"Yep," I say.

"You could appear a bit more interested." Katie scowls into the screen.

"I don't know enough. Is he gay?"

"How would I know?"

"You mean you didn't ask him?"

"It's day one. I can't be that full-on yet. Anyway, did I mention he was cute?"

"You might have, yes."

"I just think there's potential. You'll have to see. Maybe he's in one of your classes too."

"Where's he from?"

"Transferred in, according to Sam."

Sam is a girl – again, just to be clear, Katie's best friend who is a girl, as opposed to me, who is her best friend but a boy.

She continues. "She thinks his folks have moved up here with work so he had to change schools."

"I would be so pissed if that happened to me, especially in sixth form."

"Same here, but that's hardly going to happen in my home. My dad gets a nosebleed if he leaves the county."

I laugh. She is right; her dad is a homebird.

"So," I say, "no indications at all, no sign of him having had a boy-on-boy experience."

"You wish."

"Now and again."

"Is there nobody you fancy in sixth?"

"Give me a list of the gay boys and I'll let you know."

"The only one I know for defo is Cameron Black."

I choke and my face goes slightly red.

"Are you OK?"

"Cameron Black?" I get up close to the screen. "I am NOT even considering Cameron Black. Cameron Black is the gayest individual I know."

"Well, as you don't know any other gay people, that's a fairly easy thing to say."

Cameron Black minces. Not as in, he prepares a cottage pie. He wears tee-shirts that show off his tummy. Like a girl would. We are convinced he wears eyeliner. And... he calls everyone darling in a high-pitched voice, then laughs.

Save me from this Hell! I'd rather be straight.

Wait, no I wouldn't, because then I'd have to sleep with girls!

Cameron Black is looking slightly more appealing.

"There's a new girl in maths too. Think she's called Humpty or Hampton."

"Really?"

"Yeah, but I was looking more at Jamie."

"Jamie's the new guy?" I ask.

"Obvs!"

"Well, it wasn't, but it is now. Cute name, too. Maybe you should have a go at him."

Katie pulls a face.

"Sorry, that came out wrong. I meant you could ask him out."

"I'm too busy for any commitments."

"Going for a pizza isn't commitments," I object.

"One thing leads to the other."

"Doesn't have to. We could ask Sam to go too, foursome?"

Stop it!!

"Could do. Let's see how things pan out. He'll probably get snapped up, though. Did I mention he is cute?"

"No."

"Really?"

I look at my watch.

"Got to be somewhere?" she asks.

"Nope. Just wondering how things are going. You know?"

"Oh! We should go down to the restaurant and check."

"No, we most certainly should not. Can you imagine if I got a date and Dad did that?"

"Well, as you're unlikely to get a date, I wouldn't worry too much on that front."

"I guess if he isn't back before ten, we should assume it's going OK."

"Did you tell him to be back by then?" Katie chortles.

"I just told him to be careful."

"You gave him the birds and bees chat?"

"Hopefully he knows all about that. Unless I was found under a gooseberry bush."

"A gooseberry bush? This isn't 1845, you know."

"They still have gooseberry bushes now, I'll have you know."

"On that note, I need a wee," she informs me. What the connection is, I can't figure out, but we say our goodbyes and confirm we will liaise at school tomorrow and suss out 'New Guy.'

Jamie.

Cute name.

OK, so now I'm on my own I suppose you want to know more about stuff? I did promise more info on the gay quiz.

And the Doc Marten's thing.

Only it's not a thing.

Really.

It so isn't.

The short answer is that Mum and Dad asked me what I wanted for my birthday, and Freddie – he was in my form, and this was when I was fourteen – anyway, Freddie had just got a pair and I thought they were so on point. Katie said they were 'sick', which as younger readers know, is a good thing.

So, we all went online – Amazon, if you must know – and a

pair of black Doc Marten boots were purchased. I wasn't 100% certain about this but they came and I pulled them on and I loved them.

There is a sad part to this tale, though.

Ten days later, Mum died.

They were the last thing she ever bought me.

Getting emotional again.

I'm sorry, you have to bear with me.

So, they kind of became symbolic and I couldn't be parted from them.

I have three pairs now. A pair in cherry red and a pair of green ones.

I'm sure they'll be mentioned again; watch this space.

It's only 8:14pm.

I think about Dad again. I really do hope he is having a good time.

Should we have gone to the restaurant?

No, we SHOULD NOT!

To pass the time I have a shower, tidy the kitchen, and am sat at the kitchen table looking at a book called *The Little Bluebird*, which we are going to attempt in English class, when I hear the front door open.

Looking up, I see it is only 9:23pm.

Ooh!

Is this too early? Not a good sign.

Dad pokes his head around the door.

"So?" I venture. "How did your evening go?" I try to sound enthusiastic.

Dad sighs and throws his jacket onto the sofa.

Yes, we have a 'family-room-style kitchen' with a TV on the wall and a sofa, so while one of us cooks we can interact. This is another of Mum's good ideas.

I don't offer an opinion on the sigh. Let him take his time.

Does he need a hug?

Cup of tea?

He walks over to the booze cupboard and takes out a bottle of red.

Not a cup of tea, then.

"Maybe not the best evening I've ever had." He smiles, trying to make light of it.

I grimace. "That bad, huh?"

"If you like being told every financial transaction someone has ever had in their life, and how much money they have, and what they spend it on..." At this point he holds a finger up. "Sorry, no, not what they spend it on, but how they invest it, what the yields are, how you then reinvest it, then yes, it would be a great evening."

"Wow." That's all I can come up with.

"Wow," he confirms. "For GSOH, do not read Good Sense Of Humour. Read Good Salary, Own Home!"

"Wow," I say again. "At least she is financially secure by the sounds of it."

"She was humourless – didn't understand my jokes."

I suck in my teeth. Probably not that good of an idea to unload one of your jokes on a first date.

"Was she pretty?"

What am I saying? What would I know?

"In a horsey sort of a way, I suppose."

I don't even know what to say to that. I imagine she had big teeth and whinnied.

"So, not a second outing then?"

Dad pours his wine and takes a swig. "Nah. Don't think so."

"Fancy a film?"

Dad smiles.

Back to normal.

So far, so ORDINARY!

CHAPTER 2

Saturday 16th September

I am your typical teenager in that I struggle to get out of bed in the morning. It is just too warm and cosy and nice and snuggly to bother with the outside world.

I can hear Dad knocking about downstairs. Not in a bad way, no crashing of pans and slamming of cupboard doors. Just a normal Saturday.

I glance at the clock as my phone pings.

09:33.

I pick up the phone.

It's a message from Jordan. We are going shopping, or rather I am taking him shopping. He is going to his cousin's wedding in a couple of weeks and has no fashion sense.

Trust me, he does not!

Dad last night, now Jordan today. Am I the go-to fashion guru?

His mum had somehow enrolled me to take him with strict instructions on what NOT to let him buy.

I had a list.

Somewhere.

Shit, where is it?

I sit up, fully awake.

It was quite a comprehensive list. I don't know why she wasn't going with Jordan, then we would all be safe.

I remember some of the things. No Hawaiian prints, no floral, no pastels. Not jeans or shorts. Nothing that would crease. Bin bags out, then. Nothing that would catch fire. That one worries me. I'm wondering what exactly is happening at this wedding. Unless it is fireworks, which seem to be a thing at weddings now. Spend twenty grand for three minutes of crashes and flashes.

Twenty minutes later, I am showered and dressed heading down to the kitchen.

"OK?" I ask Dad as I wander in.

"Grand, thanks." Dad is wiping down the surfaces with a damp cloth. "You know, I think I realise it's not that I'm not ready for some lady action…"

Please no!

"…I just don't want any." He shrugs and moves his head slightly, side to side.

"Well, if that's what you feel then that's good," I say to him, not really knowing what else to add.

"Not to say someone might not ring my bell sometime."

Ding Dong!

"I'm heading out to meet Jordan," I tell him, grabbing a muffin.

"Is that all you're having for breakfast?"

"Nearly lunchtime," I say, glancing at the clock, which has just strolled past 10:00.

"So, I'll see you sometime? Pizza for tea if you like?"

"Great," I confirm. "What are you up to today?"

"I'm going running once I've finished up here, then I may watch the golf this afternoon."

"OK. See you later."

I retrieve my cherry-red Docs from the porch and slip them on my feet, tucking my dark blue skinny jeans in the tops. I've finished off the look with a plain royal blue tee-shirt and plenty of strappy leather bangles. One of them is quite wide, with a bronze tree fashioned out of some sort of metal. That's my favourite at the moment. Did I tell you that's my thing at the moment?

Yep, that's me, I'm gay!

I wander off towards the town centre, thinking back to when I told Jordan I was gay. Katie's reaction had been like, 'So what?' and you'll find out a bit more about what she said to me later on.

I told Katie first; that was always the rule. Any news, you told Katie first, then the rest of the world. I was pretty sure Jordan would be cool about it too, so I had planned to meet him in the park by the miniature railway, which, for information, we had ridden on like, two hundred and fifty-seven times in our younger days.

"Fancy a go on the train?" I asked him as we rounded the corner.

His face lit up. "You have to ask?"

We ended up going round twice. Even after so many rides we still saw new things or commented madly on the weird sculptures that looked as though they had been made by three-year-olds.

Then, it was time for ice cream. Huge cones with chocolate

Flakes. Jordan always ate his Flake first; I scooped up the soft white ice cream with mine until it finally melted into my mouth.

I then said to him that I had something to tell him and my mouth went dry. What if this did go totally wrong? Ten years of hanging out with this guy, doing childish things, laughing, shouting, screaming, sleepovers, being sick after too much ice cream. I didn't want to lose all that.

We were sat on a park bench with no back so he swung a leg over and sat facing me. I did likewise and we were now face to face.

Jordan pulled a face. "Nothing serious, mate? I don't do serious, or bad news, not after a ride on the train and ice cream."

"Nothing bad," I said, "but maybe a little serious."

I saw a look of horror cross his face.

Shit, just tell him.

"I like boys," I said to him.

There was a pause.

"Well, so do I," Jordan said, smiling at me.

"What?" I asked him. I hadn't seen that coming. He gave off no sense of being gay.

He continued. "I mean, I like you, and I like Ali and Shaun. Well, maybe not Shaun so much."

I sort of got where he was going with this and then realised, he hadn't fully understood my point.

"Right," I said. "OK, I don't mean as in, 'like', as you would like people generally. I mean, as in, well, I *like* boys."

Maybe I should have just said I fancy boys, or I want to sleep with a boy, or want to rip a boy's clothes off. Steady on!

"I want to hold a boy's hand. I want to kiss a boy," I added.

Jordan was blinking furiously, something he did when he was struggling to process new information.

"You want to hold my hand?" he asked me.

"No, Jordan, I love you to bits like my best friend in the world."

"Apart from Katie," he said, looking worried she might have heard me say that.

"Yeah, well, apart from Katie, but no, I don't want to hold *your* hand. That wouldn't work for us, but I'm into boys and not into girls."

There was another pause, another twitch of the eyes.

"You OK?" I asked him.

"Yeah, I'm good." Jordan didn't look happy, though.

Shit, maybe I shouldn't have told him.

"Does this mean we can't be friends anymore?" he asked me.

My heart leapt into my mouth. "Oh, shit, of course I still want to be friends, Jordan. I can't imagine ever not being friends with you. I just…" I trailed off.

Jordan gave a big sigh. "Me neither."

Yet another pause.

I wasn't handling this conversation well at all. Wasn't sure what I had expected Jordan to say, but it wasn't what he did.

He looked across at me. "So, what you're telling me is that you're gay?"

"I guess." I looked a bit sheepish.

Jordan gave a big grin. "You're my first gay friend," he announced proudly.

"So, you're OK with this?"

Jordan actually took hold of my hands in his. "Danny, I'm great with this." He looked down at our hands. "Is this OK then? Not making you feel…?"

"Feel what?" I asked. "Wrong?"

"No, you idiot. Horny!" Jordan smiled his goofy smile and I knew we were OK.

"Jordan!" I exclaimed.

"Just checking," he laughed.

Jordan is sitting on the back of a bench outside the park, the designated spot we agreed to meet.

He's in a pair of baggy shorts, showing off far too much of his underpants. A pair of Vans that should have been thrown away in year nine and some sort of floral, paisley shirt. He had turned up the short sleeves so they showed his arms off. I now get why his mum said 'no florals'; this shirt is really doing nothing for him at all. Absolutely nothing.

Whatever!

"Yo, my man." He greets me with a fist bump.

"My man," I concur. "Let's do this."

"I have a plan," Jordan announces.

Why don't I like the sound of this before I've even heard it?

"Aha?" I query.

"Pop group from the 1980s, biggest selling single Take On Me."

This is Jordan, by the way. Witty as a, well, I'll let you make your own mind up.

"Seriously," I say.

"Seriously, we go into the first shop and buy everything there. Then we have more time for larking around and throwing things about."

"No, absolutely not," I say, remembering the time he actually put this kid's scooter on the top of a van parked at traffic lights, then it drove off and to this day I still do not believe how it did not fall off! I'm not sure if the kid ever got it back. "I have a list from your mum. I will be ceremoniously killed if I do not adhere to it."

"Don't be such a scaredy cat." Jordan chortles and throws himself down from the bench, luckily hoisting his shorts at the same time or we could have had a teenage trouser incident.

"Your mum can be scary. I am entrusted with making sure you don't embarrass the rest of your family."

"Jeez, it's only a wedding." Jordan puts his arm on my shoulder and we head off.

He was so cool about me being gay and had no qualms about being touchy-feely.

And, just for the record, Jordan is SO NOT GAY!

If he was, I don't think I'd fancy him. However, he would top a poll of the most fanciable gay guys in sixth if there was only him and Cameron Black on it!

Mallington is not a huge town; there are only three clothing outlets and I plan to visit each one, make notes, get Jordan to try things on, then make an informed decision followed by a purchase. I had asked if there was a budget.

"Yes," Mrs Shelby had said. "Don't go mad!"

Jordan made out that this meant 'unlimited amounts of money'.

Hmm!

We approach Clothing4U. I never trust a shop with a number and a play on words so I don't hold out much hope of getting my boy kitted out in here. Also, my mind jumps back to Dad and his Sum Body 4U website. Could people just not use our beautiful English language properly?

Just for the record, I have never shopped here for myself. Does that make me a snob as well as being gay?

Bring it on! I'm not lowering my standards. Why am I even taking Jordan in here then? Does he not deserve better?

I turn to tell Jordan this is our first point of call and he isn't there.

"What the...?"

I twizzle round 360 degrees. Those shorts and flowery shirt are nowhere to be seen. I backtrack two shops to Vinyl Dreams, and sure enough there he is, fiddling through a rack of pop albums.

As well as having no fashion sense, his taste in music is well dubious, too. Most of the music he listens to, no-one else has even heard of.

"Have you seen they've got the 1976 copy of Wicked Albatross's Cash for Sale?" he says gleefully.

"Not interested," I say with my hands on my hips. "We are here to buy clothes."

"I'll just ask the chap behind the counter where the slacks are kept." He laughs, brandishing the album.

Yeah, well, I knew that. I knew what I meant.

"Let me just get this then you'll have my full attention."

We approach the tills and he looks at me expectantly.

"What?" I shrug.

"You've got the card."

"You mean the card for clothing purchases? Your mum's card for the purchasing of sassy wedding clothes?"

"Yeah, that's the one."

"For clothing purchases."

"I don't remember her saying that's all it was for. This is just to try and de-stress me. Today is going to be so full-on, I need something to take my mind off stuff."

"I'll do a deal with you."

That catches his attention.

"Ooh, go on."

"How about you put that back. We go and buy clothes. Then we come back and maybe I'll treat you to it."

His little face fell. "Aaaawwwww!"

I very nearly take hold of his hand like a mother would with her troublesome three-year-old to drag him out of the shop.

I just give him 'the look'.

"I'm so coming back for this," he says to the pimply assistant behind the counter.

"Sure, dude, want me to keep it for you?"

His little face lights up. How could you not love Jordan?

I close my eyes.

Don't encourage him.

Clothing 4U is a disappointment.

Jordan is desperate to get back to his Wicked Albatross so picked up the first pair of trousers through the door. Red with a black stripe down each leg on the outer side. Probably nightclubbing trousers.

I take them off him and replace them on the rack.

He fidgets about, continually hoisting his shorts.

"Maybe we'll buy you a belt too."

He heads off purposefully and picks up another pair, this time black and white check trousers.

I shake my head. Is he being deliberately obtuse?

"Oh, man, this is going to take all day," he grumbles.

"We have literally been shopping for three minutes."

"Indeed. Three minutes I'll never see again. Can we get milkshakes?"

Am I his father?

"Once we have clothes in bags," I promise.

I will probably have stern words with Mrs Shelby. I'm never doing this again.

Well, maybe not stern words.

Marks & Spencer would be a better bet. I lead him out by the elbow.

"OK, let's have a plan before we go in," I start. "How about we just get—"

"Fizz, my lad!" Jordan slaps Mark Popp on the back. Mark Popp was nicknamed Fizz for obvious reasons.

No? Fizz as in lemonade as in pop?

"Now then, boys, what are you two up to skulking down the street?"

I am very definitely NOT skulking. I am a man on a mission, walking purposefully.

"Clothes shopping," I offer.

"Oh, man," Jordan moans. "You don't have to tell everyone."

"You don't fancy milkshakes then?" Fizz asks.

No, fizzy pop!

"We do," Jordan enthuses. "Come on, let's go."

I grab his arm. "Don't you dare," I threaten him. "Let's just get this deal done then you can drink yourself stupid with milk-based products, some with a fruit-infused flavour."

Fizz sucks in his teeth and widens his eyes. He has huge brown eyes under a big mop of hair and actually... No. Stop this, Danny. We are here to buy clothes, not to find you a boyfriend!

"You don't need your mum about when he's here, do you?"

"Too true, but I'm gonna get in shit if I don't go home with new wedding clothes."

"Who's getting married?" Fizz asks. "Can anyone go?"

Really?

"Probably not. You need an invite." Jordan hops about.

Does he need the loo?

M&S is indeed a better bet. I told him in advance, plain trousers and plain shirt. Either dark trousers and a light shirt, or maybe tan trousers with a blue shirt.

I thought again about Dad last night and how smart he looked.

"Yeah," I confirm. "We are looking for tan trousers and a dark blue shirt."

"Am I not gonna look poncey in that get-up?"

"You will look a total gay! Get over it."

"Aww, man, you say the sweetest things. If I look like you, then I'll be happy."

I give him my best 'slightly irritated but in a good way' look but actually he has tugged at my heartstrings yet again. We would be the cutest couple if he was gay. Probably!

Jordan tweaks my nose playfully.

Do people actually think we are a couple?

I pick two different styles of trousers off the rails and a couple of shirts in slightly different blues, and we head over to the changing rooms.

"How many items?" asks the bored-looking girl guarding the entrance.

"Four," I tell her.

"Are you both going in?"

"Yes, I need to check he looks OK."

She looks at me in a peculiar fashion. "Really?"

"He has no fashion sense."

She looks at Jordan. "Yeah, well, I can see that."

"Cheeky." Jordan looks us both in the eye. "I *am* here, you know."

"Yes, sadly we do know. If you'd been a big boy, you could have come and done this on your own," I tell him.

"Let's get it over with." Jordan heads off in front of me. "And just for the record, I *am* a big boy."

The assistant looks from me to Jordan. "Please do not both go into the cubicle." She addresses me. "You stay outside and he can come out and show you."

"Wha... what do you think we are going to do?"

She raises her eyebrows. "You'd be surprised what people get up to. This couple last week ate their packed lunch in one of the cubicles."

I am about to complain but I can't think of the right thing to say. And anyway, Jordan already has his shorts off as they are laid on the floor.

He emerges a few moments later in his stocking feet, trousers on, shirt on but only three buttons done up and the tail hanging out of his trousers.

I fasten up all the buttons apart from the top two then move to tuck his shirt in properly.

"No!" yells the assistant. "Please let him do that himself."

Jordan stares her out. "But he's my bro, he's the man. He does everything for me."

"Not that, he doesn't," she says sternly.

I remove my hand from the front of Jordan's trousers and he looks at me and sniggers.

"Nice try, mate," he says.

"Get you later." I give him a wink.

A wink!

"What shoes will you wear?" I ask, looking at him.

"School ones."

"Aren't they black Skechers?"

"Yep."

I screw up my face. "You can't wear black shoes with tan trousers!"

"What? We need shoes too?"

"I'll go get you some. Even if you don't buy them, it will give you an idea."

"You know what size he takes?" The girl looks incredulous.

"Of course," I say, rushing past her. "Nothing I don't know about my Jordan." I give them both a backwards glance and nearly ran headlong into a rack of trousers. Very professional, Danny. Very smooth!

I come back with a pair of dark brown brogues. Maybe a bit grown-up for him, I think.

Jordan slips them on.

He actually looks better than I have ever seen him before.

I still don't fancy him, just for the record.

"Blimey," says the girl, who had now become my accomplice. "He doesn't look half bad."

"Still got it." Jordan smiles, nodding.

"You never had it," I say, "so I don't know what you think you've still got."

He opens his mouth and I give him that 'don't go there' look so he closes it again.

"You think this looks alright then?" he asks, twirling round and looking in front of the mirror at the new, improved Jordan.

"Just need a haircut," the girl says.

Tumbleweed rolls across between us and the world goes quiet. I'm sure the colour drains from my face.

"She doesn't mean it."

"Do you?" asks Jordan menacingly.

I shake my head at her.

"No, what I meant was, er, well, maybe just needs, er something," she stumbles.

"You'll be fine," I console him.

Jordan has skater-boy hair. Slightly long, blond, very unruly. All of the time. I don't even think his mum would get him to change that for the wedding. Hopefully the good job

I've done on dressing him will detract from his hair.

I'm going to be a personal shopper.

Did I tell you that?

Well, I am.

My work here is done.

Purchases in bags, including shoes, which I actually think he likes, we head off to meet Fizz for a milkshake.

Then a little voice beside me says, "You did promise me the Wicked Albatross LP."

CHAPTER 3

Monday 18th September

Officially, Sunday was boring. Nothing happened, so skip to Monday. That's the good thing about telling a story, you don't have to live through the boring bits.

I am excited at the prospect of seeing the new boy.

I don't have to wait long, as it happens.

I walk into the sixth form common room. Apparently as everyone in sixth form is at the very least sixteen going on seventeen, we can now be trusted with comfy chairs and a coffee machine. Still feels a bit weird having a room where we can escape the younger kids, and as rooms go this isn't too bad. As I say, there's a coffee machine and comfy chairs and even now, early in the morning there are a few other students about, drinking coffee from said machine, reading, chatting about the weekend, lounging about.

Katie comes in and plonks down in the chair opposite me.

"Want a coffee?" she asks.

"Nah." I didn't drink coffee before sixth form so I'm not going to start now just because it's on offer, although to be honest you only get coffee after putting your cash in the slot at the top.

Before she has a chance to go for her coffee, she raises a hand and calls out, "Jamie, come and meet Danny."

I jump up, way too enthusiastically, knock my book to the floor, tip the contents of my bag out and catch my toe on the leg of the chair, putting me off balance, so I reached out awkwardly. Nice move, Danny. I'm trying to scrabble about and collect my belongings as Jamie comes into view.

Wow and double wow!

I could have done with the support of something steady.

"Hey," he calls out, raising his hand and making his way over.

Gorgeous teeth as he smiles a gorgeous smile.

Close-cropped hair, which I wouldn't normally go for, and when he smiles, combined with his big brown eyes everything just works so well. A butterfly twists in my tummy momentarily.

He has skinny blue jeans that fit everywhere they are supposed to, plain black tee-shirt and black and white trainers.

So understated, as if it has taken no effort at all to conjure up this look.

So bloody gorgeous.

He is standing quite close. I notice we are similar in height. A good height, Gramps always says when he sees me. I imagine kissing him.

Really?

Really! I wouldn't have to bend down, neither would he. We would be a perfect fit.

What?

Why do I always do this with new kids?

Stop. Right. Now!

There's that butterfly again, trying to get out of my chest.

Katie has her arm around my shoulder. I try unsuccessfully to shake it off. I don't need to give him the wrong impression.

Like, Katie and I are not together. He needs to know that.

What am I doing? He won't be gay.

Sure?

Positive. He gives off manly vibes.

Stop thinking, Danny!

Just, totally stop thinking this out!

Katie introduces us. "This is Danny. We've known each other, like, forever."

"Good to meet you, Danny." Jamie thrusts out his hand.

Very grown-up!

I shake his hand. Nice firm grip, warm, gorgeous.

"Likewise. Seems everyone has met you apart from me. I must have had my head under a stone last week."

I want to add 'LOL'. Luckily, I don't.

Holy crap, this guy is hot. This will probably be the first and last time I get to talk to him. The girls are going to be all over this hottie.

Katie asks Jamie if he would like a coffee. He would. I thought I would be sent off to get it but she tells us to sit down and she will fetch it.

She gives me a look that says, 'Katie has a plan.'

"All a bit mental, really," he says.

I nod. "Yeah, our own coffee machine. What's that about then?" I laugh a little nervously.

Calm. The. Fuck. Down.

He's only a boy.

OK, a bloody gorgeous boy.

"What are you studying?" he asks genuinely.

"Maths, English and history."

"Oh, right, I'm maths and history too. Economics is my third. We might be in the same set for stuff? That would be cool."

Would it?

Er, yes, Danny. Keep up!

Jamie gets out his timetable to check. It appears we are in the same maths and history sets.

"Oh, I thought you were in Katie's set for maths." I look puzzled but then clam up. It would look as if Katie had said something to me about him being in her set.

"Really?" Jamie looks quizzically at us both, wondering if we have been talking about him, no doubt, and yes, Jamie, you would be right. We have indeed been talking about you. "I was apparently put in the wrong set and have been moved. Does it mean we are thicker than Katie?" he laughs.

"Nope," Katie says. "When it comes to maths, I can add seven to four and get twelve quite easily. So, you are both officially brighter than Katie."

We all laugh.

How am I going to get through this day without talking gibberish? I may be relatively bright but I'm also a huge romantic and can make stories up out of nothing. Sometimes I voice things I should keep to myself. This is going to be so hard!

History is first up today.

You could not have planned this.

I keep telling myself to get a bloody grip. But then I keep

telling myself dreams are cheap.

Yeah, mate, this is seriously just a dream.

"OK?" Jamie asks.

"Huh?"

"You seemed to disappear off into the distance." He gives a laugh.

Concentrate, Danny!

"Fine, yeah, I'm fine." Apart from being a total wreck. Stop looking so bloody gorgeous, stop smiling that gorgeous smile.

Is it just me who can see this? No-one else is visibly fawning over Jamie. It is obviously just me. But, like, how? Jamie is acting so normal in front of us all. He isn't a gibbering wreck, which equates to straight as a die.

Katie comes to my rescue and thrusts a plastic cup into Jamie's hand. "Can't guarantee it will taste like something from Costa!"

"I'd be very surprised if it does," Jamie says. "You not drinking, Danny?"

"No, I'm sad when it comes to coffee," I say.

But you could cheer me up.

Jamie looks a little confused at my choice of sentence. Why didn't I just say, 'No, I don't drink coffee'? That, after all, was the question.

Katie looks at me as if to say, 'What the fuck?'

I count to ten in my head and try again. "Sorry, I mean I don't drink coffee. Where have you transferred in from then?" I hear myself ask, moving the chat away from hot drinks.

"Basingstoke. Mum's job brought her north, had to come with her."

"Wow, quite a way away."

"Yeah, but I have to admit it's lovely up here. We came up a couple of weeks ago to get settled."

I could have shown him round had I known.

"Shame I hadn't known you guys then. You could have shown me round."

Really?

What the actual?

Is he verbalising my thoughts?

Have to be careful from now on, Danny!

"That would have been so cool," Katie chirped. "We can still show you stuff. If you like."

"Yeah, that sounds like a plan," he says. That smile!

First bell sounds.

"OK then, Danny, lead the way."

I could have done with some time with Katie before heading off to a lesson with Jamie. I could have done with her telling me firstly to calm down, then say nothing stupid, then do nothing stupid, then, well, then just, oh, I don't know!

Katie gives me a thumbs-up as I glance round.

We walk along the corridor to the lesson. I should be chatting to him, general stuff, anything, but if I open my mouth, I'm going to tell him I love him or something equally stupid. I've known him for like, sixteen minutes. You cannot possibly fall in love in sixteen minutes. Can you?

History goes by in a bit of a blur. Jamie takes the seat next to me, second row back by the windows.

Doesn't ask.

Is that cheeky?

Do I care?

You bet not! But then I get to thinking, and it seems, well, he doesn't know anyone else in history so maybe I am the easy option. We had been chatting, after all, when the bell went. But how did he know I don't usually sit next to someone else who might be a bit miffed to see me with a new gorgeous-looking guy?

Again... Bothered? Not!

And then...

End of the lesson...

Miss Halshaw says, "OK, historians," her little joke, "we will be undertaking a small project for a few weeks on the history of the landscape garden. You will work in pairs. Please come with your partner to the next lesson all geared up to be brilliant."

Before I get a chance, Jamie asks, "You fancy partnering up?"

"Er, yes, that would be fine," I stutter, but somehow it doesn't come out at all enthusiastically.

I think he picks up on it. "Sorry, that's being very presumptuous of me. I guess you usually go with someone else on these things."

"To be honest there's only two others here that I have been with before in history and I don't fancy either of them."

Pause.

Really?

Been with before?

Fancy?

"Sorry, I don't mean fancy as in, well, you know." I can feel my face going red. My day is going so brilliantly.

Jamie laughs and squeezes my shoulder. "Hey, I know what you meant. That's cool then. History Buds?"

"Sure." I don't squeeze him back. Somehow it doesn't seem right, yet he managed it effortlessly and made it look like the most natural thing in the world.

I have a history buddy.

I feel totally cool about that.

There's that butterfly again.

And, so, obviously I will get to speak to Jamie again, at least in history, which by the way will be totally fine. I can cope with that.

I just hope I can start acting like a mature human being instead of a neanderthal who has just emerged from the sludge and doesn't yet speak English!

"History buddies?" Katie asks, clapping wildly.

"Yeah, and I didn't suggest it, he did."

"So how do you feel about that?"

"Fine," I lie, acting cool. I couldn't be less cool, even though it was exactly what I wanted. Jamie all to myself.

"Well, that's a good start. You'll have him in your bed by next Friday."

I swivel round and hiss at her. "Stop already. That is so not going to happen." I know it isn't going to happen but as I said earlier, probably three pages back, or so, dreams are cheap. At the moment this one is free.

Jordan waltzes over. "Hey, guys, how is living the high life in Common Room 3 going?"

'Do not mention any of this,' I mouth to Katie.

"Danny has a history buddy," she proudly announces.

Like, what just happened?

"What's a history buddy?" Jordan asks. "I can only start imagining stuff that is not going to be in anyone's head but my own, so please enlighten me, very quickly."

"There's a hot new guy in town, and our Danny has managed to hook up with him."

OK, so he is hot.

I have NOT hooked up with him!

Jordan straddles a chair, back to front. "You. Absolute. Tart. Spill the beans. What do you have to do with your history buddy?" Jordan holds a finger up. "Quick now, before I start imagining things again."

"It's just a history project. In history."

"Yeah." Katie clicks her tongue. "We grasped that, mister."

"Do you have to do stuff after school?" Jordan asks. "Like in each other's bedrooms?"

What is wrong with these people?

"Stop! Nothing will be happening in anyone's bedroom." Maybe I voice that a little loudly.

"You wish, stud," says Melissa from a row behind.

"Now look, the whole common room will know in a minute."

"And, your problem is?" Katie smiles.

"Please, let's just drop it." I say, getting up and throwing my Pepsi can in the recycling bin. I turn. "I need to be somewhere." I head off, leaving them open mouthed.

I lean up against the wall outside the common room.

What the fuck is wrong with me?

I never, ever, but never, feel like this.

I am rational, I am sensible, I am grown-up, I am not thirteen, however...

I have a history buddy. Bedrooms were mentioned.

Get. A. Grip!

An onion-based smell hits me as I open the front door after school. Dad is cooking onions. No shit, Sherlock!

"Mmmmmm, something smells good," I say, walking into the kitchen where he is stirring something in a frying pan.

"Thought I'd do a bolognaise. OK?" he asks without turning.

"Great, thanks." I grab a can from the fridge. "Anything I can do?"

"All good, thanks. You could set the table, but it will be a while yet."

I was always good at getting out of school uniform, loved to feel free of school, but since sixth form started and we can wear our own choice of clothes, I had been getting home and staying in what I was in. So, I just lounge on the large, deep sofa at the back of the family room, looking through some of my stuff from school today.

"Getting settled into sixth form then?" Dad asks.

"Yeah, still seems strange having a designated place to go to between lessons and everything seems a lot freer."

"Well, I suppose you've chosen to be there now, rather than having to go. They treat you like adults. Any new people?"

Has someone been talking?

"A few," I say casually. "I seem to have got myself tagged with a new guy in history for a project we have to do."

"OK with that?"

Remind me again if I was OK with that.

"Yeah, he seems fine. Transferred up from somewhere down south as his folks have moved jobs, or something."

"What's the project about?"

"Hm," I pause, knowing what is coming, "History of landscape gardening."

"Oh wow!" Dad says.

That was what Mum had done. She went round designing other people's gardens and she had been to college after I was born to study that.

"You know, all Mum's stuff is in the attic if you need to look at anything."

"Will that be OK though?"

"Why not? If she was here," Dad gives a small gulp, "she would have wanted you to use it."

"Sure."

"See how it goes," he says.

I change the subject.

"So, heard anything from Evie?"

"Just a one-line text."

I wait.

"No-go," he adds, bashing the wooden spoon round the pan.

That's the end of that, then.

Or is it?

"Thought I might re-jig my profile." More bashing.

Didn't he say maybe he wasn't ready for any lady action? I cringe at the fact I thought about that again.

"OK. Need any help?"

"I'll shout if I do. I worry that Katie had bigged me up too much."

Hm.

"Maybe now you're in sixth you will find someone."

Where is all this coming from?

"Plenty of time, Dad. I need to concentrate on my studies. Katie is enough to handle anyway and everyone would have to be vetted by her."

"Good luck with that, Danny!"

"Indeed. I'm sure she'll advise me when someone comes along that she thinks is suitable."

I guess Katie is, at this very moment, sat at her desk in her pink bedroom, favourite pen in hand, fluffy animal character on the top of it, making notes about what has happened today.

I smile as I think back to today. Meeting Jamie was pretty cool. I remembered us sitting together in history, him asking questions about stuff, seeming so relaxed. If I'd been the new boy, I would have been ultra shy, very quiet and not saying much at all. Jamie does come across as a confident person, and I think he will fit in great. I just hope I can at least remain friends with him and not get lost along the way as time goes by.

One thing I remember telling Jordan when I came out to him was that I liked holding a boy's hand. I hadn't actually done that yet. Apart, of course, from when Jordan grabbed my hands and then asked if it made me horny! I guess I would really like to do it and so I fantasised a lot about how it would feel.

Has someone come along that might just be suitable?

Katie seems to be encouraging me, even though I am still 99% certain Jamie has no interest in boys. He's doing some after-school football thing tonight, and yes, I know you're going to say gay boys can play football, but somehow he doesn't fit the profile. I'll just have to bide my time.

Not looking, OK?

CHAPTER 4

Tuesday 19th September

Still not looking, OK!

So why am I making such an effort to look appealing and attractive? I've never had such a dilemma about what to wear for school.

For school, FFS!

For sixth, even. Now I'm calling it school again!

I've even had two different pairs of jeans on.

This is ridiculous.

I stick to blue jeans and a grey hoodie. I lace up my black DM 1460s and grab my bag. Dad has already left so I shout out, "See you later, folks. Love you, Mum."

It's something I do when I know there's only me. My eyes prick with tears.

Katie, Sam, and Jordan are sat on one of the picnic benches outside the sixth form common room. Every school seems to have picnic benches now. I wonder if it's to try and get us pasty-faced teens to sit in the sunshine. The sun is shining today and it's actually quite warm.

"Hey," we all say to each other, the generic greeting for

sixteen-year-olds.

Who knew?!

"Forgot to tell you," Jordan starts. "Mum thinks you're amazing."

"Well, I always knew that," I say.

"To be fair, he's right," Katie says. "He always knew that."

"Why am I particularly amazing today?"

"Well, I should have texted you on Saturday. Mum says the clothes you got me are spot on. Just the sort of thing a sixteen-year-old would wear to a wedding."

Sam looks up from her book. "What have you been buying him?"

"Just some trousers and a shirt."

"And shoes. Proper shoes. Never had proper shoes." Jordan looks down at his black Skechers.

Sam laughs. "You're going to look like a proper adult. You have to send us pictures."

Jordan's face drops.

"What's up?" I ask him.

"I'm not ready to be a proper adult yet."

"Just for one day. Break yourself in gently," I add, rubbing his arm.

"You are so like a married couple," Sam says, burying her head in her book.

"Nah, he's— Ow! What was that for?"

Katie had kicked him under the bench.

She obviously hasn't mentioned Jamie to Sam; however, Sam is engrossed in her novel so doesn't realise the significance of the kick.

Katie gives Jordan a look.

Jordan holds up his hands as first bell sounds.

Katie links arms with me. "Any lessons with newbie Jamie today?" she asks.

"Yeah, maths this afternoon."

"Get him to sit next to you."

"I can't just do that," I object, although the thought makes me feel warm inside and once again loosed the butterfly in my chest.

As it happens, I don't need to worry on that front. It would appear everyone is conspiring to pull Jamie and me together, even if nothing comes of it apart from a good friendship, which to be honest I will settle for.

I walk into maths. Jamie is already there standing by Miss Wilson's desk, discussing something.

"Ah, Danny, just the man." Miss Wilson beckons me over. Jamie smiles that smile at me. She looks up at Jamie. "Danny is our maths guru. He can work out any equation faster than anyone in class so I'd like him to be your guru too."

I look at her quizzically.

"Jamie's last school did things a bit differently and he needs to be shown line segments before we crack on with the co-ordinate geometry."

"Oh, I get it now," I say. Miss Wilson and I have a good relationship, probably because I'm her star pupil. "Save you the bother."

"I couldn't have put it better myself," she says. "You'll be able to explain it better than me anyway."

I feel a little bit awkward. Does Jamie think I'm a swot? Maybe he doesn't want a clever-arse friend. However, he looks at me as if holding me in high esteem.

"I'm not that good," I stutter. "I just find it, well, you know."

"Easy?" asks Jamie.

"It just comes naturally to him," Miss Wilson continues. "So, please sit together. We are just going through the term syllabus today so after that the rest of the lesson will be yours to explain how it all works."

I get to sit next to Jamie again?

We take our seats.

"Sorry about all this," Jamie says. "I don't want to cause any bother. I'll try to be a quick learner."

"No bother at all," I say in a jolly manner. This will indeed be no bother at all. I get Jamie all to myself for two hours. I need to concentrate, though, as I am supposed to be helping him to find the mid-point of a line segment, among other things.

Then he continues, "People will be starting to talk." He laughs. "We seem to be getting stuck with each other at every turn."

I gulp. I'm not ready for this yet. However, I wouldn't say I'm being 'stuck with' Jamie. I hope he doesn't think he is being stuck with me and I'm just an easy fix for his needs... Mathematical needs, of course!

Thirteen minutes later and Miss Wilson has skipped through the syllabus and is now eating a chocolate digestive while flicking through something on her desk.

"OK, shall we make a start?" I ask.

"I feel like I'm in the presence of a superstar," Jamie says.

"Stop already," I say. "She doesn't know what she's saying."

I flick open the old GCSE coursebook and we make a start. I have to say I find this so easy, I just hope I can explain it in a way that Jamie will understand too. Why am I doubting him?

He probably knows this stuff backwards, just not in the way we were taught it.

I then realise I am sitting staring at the page and not saying anything.

"Sorry, just wondering how to start," I bluff.

"I am entirely in your hands." Jamie smiles again.

I wish!

Jamie is actually fine with all this; he soon picks stuff up and repeatedly says things like, "Oh yeah, we did this the other way round." Or, "That makes so much more sense the way you explain it."

I have to say there are times when I feel slightly giddy at the close proximity of him. At one point he reaches his hand over mine to point at something I have written and ask a question. I almost feel a surge of electricity jumping between our fingers. I move my hand away slightly, not wanting to, well, I'm not sure what I'm not wanting but it feels right somehow. Then a few minutes later he is pointing at something with his pencil and it slips out of his hand, and after landing on the back of my hand rolls to a stop by my little finger. Jamie instinctively reaches for it and our fingers touch. Only briefly, like a millisecond of time but I feel it standing still and part of me wishes the pencil was under my hand so he would have to pick it up to retrieve it.

I move my hand away again so he can pick his pencil up.

"Yikes, I'm a butterfingers today."

I'm quiet for a bit then say, "Yikes, that's a great word, haven't heard it in ages."

Jamie looks at me and laughs. "Could it be a southern thing?"

"Darn would be more southern," I counter.

"Wouldn't that be the deep south in America?" Jamie laughs again.

I blush again, hoping he isn't conscious of my skin changing colour every time I speak.

The lesson is over in a flash, or so it seems, and that is probably the end of our sitting together. My work here is done.

Again, I don't need to worry on that front.

"Maybe I can sit with you all the time," Jamie says. "If I get stuck, I can ask my guru. Or is that being too, well, you know."

I don't know exactly. Too forward?

"That would be great," I say honestly.

Truthfully.

Truly.

Wonderfully.

Miss Wilson breaks in on my reverie.

"OK Jamie? How did that go?"

"I see what you mean, Miss," he says.

"Told you."

Then to me. "You know if I was ever off sick, I could rely on you to take the class, Danny."

"Pah," I say.

She pulls a face.

Jamie laughs. I love to hear him laugh.

Katie and I walk home together. Jamie has another football thing, which he tells me he would really rather not be doing but sort of got pulled into it by some of the guys in his economics class.

"So," I start but then pause.

"So?" Katie looks across at me.

"There's so much Jamie does that makes me think that he might like me, a bit more than, you know."

"I know," she says. "Anything in particular?"

"I can't put my finger on it."

"But you'd like to?" Katie sniggers.

"Behave!" I scowl. "He's just so gentle, he listens and seems to be interested in what I say, he's always saying stuff then apologising as if he thinks he's said the wrong thing. A straight guy wouldn't think twice."

We walk on for a bit.

"Are you just going to have to ask him? Maybe tell him you are gay and see what response that gets?"

"Yeah, but, I'm just so worried that he won't want to still be friends at all if I tell him. I am just enjoying the 'matey' thing we've got going and don't want it to end." I stop in my tracks. "Not sure if he would be as cool as Jordan about stuff."

"You're happy to be 'matey'?" she asks. "Not a very 'gay' word to use."

I have to admit, in the short time we have known each other he has never called me 'mate.' He always uses my name, which is great. "What else can I call it at the moment?" I ask her.

"But don't you worry that the longer you don't say anything, the worse he will react when you do tell him?"

"Oh, why does life have to be so confusing at times?" I feel like wailing.

"Have you asked him about his previous life? See if you can find out if he left a girlfriend behind. Or a boyfriend!"

Katie gives me a slightly evil look.

I sigh. "It seems everything I wish for regarding Jamie is working out. Maybe I should wish him to be gay? I mean, you said I should get him to sit next to me, then Miss Wilson says we have to. Then at the end of the lesson I'm thinking, well, that was nice but he'll drift off to his own place now, and he suggests we sit together in future."

Katie grabs my arm and pulls me to a stop. "You never mentioned this before," she says excitedly. "It has to be a sign."

"No, it just means he doesn't know anybody else in maths and we sort of got shoved together and maybe he sees me as a free ride."

"Bollocks. He likes you, plain as." Katie pulls me on again and we step out towards the crossing where we drift off our separate ways.

"Let's see where it goes. I'm not in a class with him tomorrow."

Katie stops by the crossing and looks me in the face. "I'm going to make some notes and have a good think about things tonight and see if we can't get something moving along."

"Oh, please, no. Don't be suggesting something silly."

"Silly? Me?" Katie gives a chuckle and presses the crossing button. "See you in the morning."

I watch her take the crossing and fear for my sanity.

I lay on my bed, trying to do some reading ready for English tomorrow but I couldn't get my mind off Jamie and Katie. Jamie in a good way, Katie in a slightly worried, panicky, scared way. It could go one of two ways, either she would get bored and the whole thing would fizzle out, or, well, it didn't bear thinking about.

My phone pings.

Katie

Blind date?

Me

Sorry?

Katie

You and Jamie.

I cannot guess where this is going. Neither of us, as far as I'm aware, are on a dating site, or maybe he is. Has Katie seen something?'

Me

What have you seen?

Katie

Nothing. Just thought we could set something up. Make it look like you were meeting someone else but we get Jamie to be there.

Me

Where?

Katie

I don't know. Don't rush things.

Me

Then stop before you start. I knew this would get out of hand horribly. Just leave things, Katie. I need to think.

Katie

Pah! You're rubbish. You'll just let it fester.

Yeah, like a scab, I thought.

Katie

Ok, catch you later.

And she is gone, like a whirlwind, as she arrived.

I throw my book down; no chance of anything sinking in now. Maybe I need to take the upper hand. Do something slightly less stupid than Katie would have done.

But what?

I've thought about boys before but don't think I've ever felt like this about one. What is it exactly that is making me feel this way? Before I can answer myself my phone pings again.

"FFS, Katie," I groan as I pick it up.

Jamie

Thx 4 2day.

Followed by a smiley emoji.

Crap! It's from Jamie! Where has he got my number from? I haven't given him it. Have I? Have I been so out of it that I don't even remember?

I sit up on the bed, heart pounding. What do I say? You're welcome? It was my pleasure? Kisses? Heart?

I start to type, 'no problem'.

Really? Is that the best you can do, Danny Ross? I backspace and start again.

Me

It was my pleasure. You're a great student.

That sounded better, not too over the top. I clicked send.

I was thanked with three LOL emojis.

Is that it? I wait. Then I wait some more. I check my phone has signal. Is he waiting for me to comment on three emojis? What do I say to three emojis? 'Are you gay?' No, I don't even type that because I know if I do I will click send accidentally and that will be that.

Do I ask him how he feels he is getting on, is he settling in? OMG, Katie and I can text for England without taking breath, but this is so hard. Maybe I just leave it at that.

Katie would beat me up if she knew I had an opening and didn't take advantage of it.

Jamie

What are you up to tonight?

I almost drop my phone.

Now that makes it easier. A question I can answer, and no, I wasn't about to say I was thinking of him.

Me

Just trying to do some reading for English tomorrow.

Jamie

Soz, did I disturb you?

Me

Not at all. Glad of the distraction.

So far so good.

Jamie

Happy to oblige.

Jamie texts back with another smiley emoji. He seems keen on emojis. I will hook him up with Jordan, who tries to send all his messages in emoji without text. The other night he was eating in his bedroom and he sent a picture of a boy with a banana in bed. He didn't seem to be worried about the symbolism it could have conjured up.

Me

How about you?

Jamie

Mum just doing T. Hanging for that.

Me

Dad cooking here too, think it's leftover bolognaise.

Jamie

Oh stop!

Me

What did I say?

Jamie

Mum making baked aubergine something.

Why can't I be having bolognaise?

Is there room at yours for a little one?

More laughing emojis from Jamie.

Always room for a little one here, I think fondly.

I send a shocked emoji. Two can play at the emoji game.

Jamie

Tea ready, gotta go.

Me

OK, thanks for the thanks.

That feels a bit stupid but I send it.

Jamie

Catch you tomorrow.

And he is gone.

I had the opportunity there to invite him round for tea and I ballsed it up. I always think of things after the moment has gone.

I have two options. Text Katie and tell her all about it, or, option two, don't tell her anything and just do some reading.

"Tea, Danny."

Or, option three, go and have tea. That sounds like a better plan!

For now, anyway. Gives me chance to think.

CHAPTER 5

Thursday 21st September

Why does Jamie look so damn perfect in whatever he wears? Today he has a denim shirt on, with black jeans and grey Converse hi-tops. He has had a different outfit on every day. I bet his mother loves all the laundry he creates. I could tell you what he has worn every day this week.

Am I a freak?

Possibly, yes!

"I love that you wear DMs," Jamie says, sitting down.

It's history again, the start of being History Buddies.

"Really?" I ask. "Thanks. I suppose it's just my look."

"They look great on you." He kicks at my boot with one of his Converse trainers and smiles.

It's like he sends a shock up my leg, in a good way of course.

"I sometimes wish I had a look," he continues.

"Well, you sort of do. I mean we all sort of do, don't we? That sounds mad now I've said it!"

What was I saying? Would he pick up on it?

"Should I get some?" he asks.

"If you like. I think they're amazing. I've got three pairs." I then add for good measure, "If you're my size you could always try them on and see what you think."

What was I saying? Again!

I instantly imagine him wearing my cherry-red DMs. Oh, that's a nice thought. No! Not nice!! That is a bloody amazing, hot thought.

Shit! I'm going to be in trouble in a moment. Calm down, Danny Boy!

"Have you always worn them? Or is it a sixth thing?" he goes on to ask.

"A couple of years." Then before I know it, I'm saying, "Mum bought them for me."

"Your mum is way too cool." He laughs.

"Sorry, I should have said." I falter and pause. "What I meant to say is…" The words trail off.

He picks up on my distress. "Shit, did I say something?"

"No, I just, well I – I should have said my mum died. I shouldn't have mentioned her, I suppose." I look up tearfully. "It's not your fault," I gabble on.

"Oh, Danny, that's bloody awful. I'm so sorry." He really doesn't know what to do and it's not his fault. Then he reaches out and simply puts his hand on my arm, then after a moment I wonder if he thinks better of it and gently removes his hand to a safe distance.

Why did I mention that Mum bought them? That gave him an opening to make a comment about her, which then led to… well, to this.

He reaches into his bag and pushes a pack of tissues across the desk, trying to not make it obvious. He turns sideways to shield me and my stupid tears. His thoughtfulness makes me want to cry full-on.

I look down at the desk and rub away the tears.

Jamie squeezes my arm again, another contact. Did he have second thoughts about his action and now believes that a gentle touch is better than no contact at all? "I'll shut up. If you want to tell me later about your mum, please do."

"Thanks," I say, looking up at him.

Awkward.

"I've worn them ever since," I add. "Sort of like a tribute and I feel good when I wear them."

"No other reason needed. I think that's lovely."

"Good morning, historians," pipes Miss Halshaw as she blows into the room.

"Good morning, Miss," we all reply.

"So, this little project…" And she's off.

Just as well, really, it gives me time to compose myself before we have to speak to each other again.

"…so, you can stay here in class, go to the library, common room, or whatever to make a start."

Jamie looks at me and takes the lead. "Let's get out of here," he says quietly.

We end up at one of the picnic benches, no-one else around.

"I'm sorry," I blurt out as we take a seat. "It's so pathetic, every time I—"

"Danny, do not EVER apologise for feeling like this. I can't begin to imagine how you must feel losing your mum." Jamie's tone is so gentle. A guy I have literally known for less than a week. He could have just turned away in class, not knowing how to deal with a flake like me. I just want to throw my arms around him and cry myself stupid.

"It's not as if it was yesterday, though," I say. "It's nearly two years."

"Doesn't mean you have to be over it or moved on," Jamie says. "She must have been very special and you will always have moments like this. Don't feel it's wrong."

I don't know this guy but...

"I know we don't really know each other yet," Jamie starts, then is a bit unsure of what to say. I suppose he doesn't want to make it sound crass or... whatever.

Jamie smiles at me. "She had great taste in footwear anyway."

I smile back and the tension is gone.

"Yeah, and what's more, she was a landscape gardener. She's going to get us an A in this project."

"Brilliant, because did I say I don't do anything less than an A. I was worried you might not be up to the challenge."

I cough. "Not up to the challenge? Careful what you wish for, I'll be watching you!"

Back to normal.

This guy is phenomenal. Even if Jamie is not gay, I will love him forever.

I lie on my bed feeling emotionally drained. So many thoughts whirling around in my head. Yet again, I had lost it a bit thinking about Mum, but Jamie had said it was fine, and it probably was. The thing is, I don't want to get emotional every time I think about Mum. I can only remember good things when I think about her so why can't I smile when I mention her? I had concealed the day's events from everyone. I don't need Katie giving me a big hug, or worse still, thinking something into me and Jamie that isn't there. I also haven't mentioned anything to Dad; he would be just as bad as me and we'd end up crying together. He really is such a softie. I seriously cannot see him with anyone else.

But then my head is in turmoil again at how sweet Jamie was, and his actions. A double arm squeeze, caring, tissues at the ready. I'm not feeling confused, at least I don't think I am, but I do feel like there is a message there somewhere in what happened.

My phone pings.

Katie

You dashed off today. Ok?

Me

Yeah, all good x

Trust her to notice.

Katie

Any developments?

This meant, 'Any news on Jamie?'

Me

Good session in history (winking emoji)

Yes! Winking!!

My phone pings.

Jordan

Wotcha doing gayboy?

Remind me why I am friends with Jordan!

Me

Laid on my bed dreaming of you.

Jordan

Aaw sweet.

Katie

So nothing happening with you two?

Not ready to tell her of today's developments, I decide.

Me

Nope

Katie

Jordan and me have a plan

Jordan

Katie and me have a plan

OMG. What are the chances? I think things are moving pretty well without any intervention on their part.

I wish Jordan would grasp the use of a WhatsApp group. It would be so much easier for us to communicate than having to text the same stuff back and forth to each other, but it was just one thing he could not get his head around.

Me to both

Ok?

Katie and Jordan

Bake brownies

I smile to myself.

Me to both again

Ok, and?

Jordan

Invite him round to do buddy stuff

Katie

Sometimes Danny you can be frustrating!

Me to Katie

That's what you love about me.

Katie

Sometimes I wonder why.

Me to Katie

Things are ok as they are at the moment.

Jordan

You still there?

Me to Jordan

Yeah, Katie bending my ear.

Jordan

No shit.

Katie

You ignoring me now?

Me to Katie

Nope, having a three way with you and Jordan, have patience.

Katie

Tell him to do one.

My phone pings.

Jamie!

Hey history buddy, just checking in. You ok?

Ooh!

Me to Jamie

Yeah, bit of an emotional day but I'm fine.

Jamie

Good, I was worried

A bit worried

Not paranoia!

I smile. Jamie so deserved to be gay, then I could love him a little bit! Well, a little bit more than I already do.

Katie

You are ignoring me.

Why are you texting Jordan more than me?

Jordan

Aren't I not as important as Katie?

Me to both

You are super important to me, but don't make me choose!

Jamie

Sorry, guess you are busy, just wanted to, you know, check.

Me to Jamie

Sorry, Jordan and Katie texting too, bit manic.

Jamie

I'll let you chat to them, just wanted to check.

Me to Jamie

No, you don't have to go.

Katie

I can't wait around for texts though. Needs to be back, forth, back, forth.

Me to Katie

Chill.

Have you not had a good day?

Jordan

I was only joking. You're my gay bestie. Love you man.

Jamie

Just re-read my texts. Paranoia! Sorry

Katie

No, sorry, love you loads.

Me to Katie

Love you loads too. Thanks for being there for me.

Me to Jordan

Love you too man.

Jamie

You are welcome. I think (weird head emoji)

What did that mean?

Katie

You do love me back. Right?

Me to Katie

Yeah of course. Just said so didn't I?

Katie

No!

I sit up.

I scrolled back through my messages to her.

Nope, I hadn't said it.

Maybe I pressed delete instead of send?

Oh, shit!

I opened up Jamie.

There it is.

'Love you loads too. Thanks for being there for me.'

No no no no no no no!

Me to Katie

Shit!

Katie

What?

Me to Katie

I sent this to Jamie instead of you …… Love you loads too. Thanks for being there for me.

Crap!

Katie

How?

Me to Katie

Because I'm texting all three of you at the same time.

Me to Jamie

Sorry Jamie, that was meant for Katie, I can't text to more than one person at a time. I always cock up!

Katie

Sorry!

I'll go, sort it out

I'll text Jordan, tell him to leave you be.

Jamie

Shame.

Eh? What does that mean? I scroll back. Did it mean he wished the message was for him? That I loved him? But I said 'I love you TOO'. He hadn't said he loved me.

Aaargh!

Lighten it up!

Me to Jamie

Well I do love everyone, so it can be for you too.

Jamie

(Heart emoji)

Oh, wow!

What?

Really?

Jamie

Sorry, that was inappropriate.

I was going to ask if you wanted to do some project work

Me to Jamie

Absolutely

You can come here if you like?

Or I can come to you?

Jamie

Don't mind. It's probably quieter at yours. Mum gets a bit full on!

I laugh to myself.

Me

That's fine.

Weekend?

Jamie

Or Friday after school?

Me

Sorry, Gramps is coming for tea

Jamie

Ok, Saturday is great then.

Tea ready, gotta go. Chat at school.

BTW sorry for being weird

Not sure what he is apologising for.

Me

No problem, see you tomorrow

Jamie

Night (sleepy emoji)

I reply in the same vein then fall back on my pillow. What an intense exchange of texts.

Maybe he is just like Jordan, happy to have a gay buddy. But wait, he doesn't know I'm gay. Has he guessed? Maybe he's just lonely and likes me and because we are doing stuff together in maths and history it's an easy option.

Aaargh again!

CHAPTER 6
Friday 22nd September

I feel mentally drained this morning with yesterday's weirdness in school and associated texts, but also super excited because Gramps is coming for tea.

Gramps is Mum's dad, so he is extra special because he is someone who still gives me that link with her, and he is the coolest Gramps you could wish to have. He will be seventy next year but certainly doesn't act it. He has a big silver beard, which he is so proud of, with a curling moustache and is a bit of a fashionista, wearing waistcoats and a variety of hats. He is just so well turned out.

Oh, yes, and he usually brings me the most wonderful gifts at special times.

That puts a smile on my face as I leave the house.

I feel that as I walk through the gates at school, I will certainly have three sets of eyes on me with different questions all lined up to fire at me.

Yep. Got that right.

The good thing – is it a good thing? – is that Jamie, Katie, and Jordan are all sat together at one of the benches. I wonder if they have been chatting. Has anything been said about yesterday? I'm pretty sure Jamie won't have said anything about the episode in class and I'm pretty sure Katie won't have said anything about knowing that I sent a text meant for her to Jamie.

But hey, let's find out!

"Hey," I greet the gathered clan.

A chorus of, "Hey," is returned.

I slink onto the bench next to Katie, opposite the boys. My boys! I'm thinking it would have been easier had there been only Jamie, or only Katie and Jordan; it's all a bit quiet.

Katie as usual breaks the ice. "How are you this lovely morning?"

"I'm good, thanks. Gramps coming tonight for tea so can't wait for that."

"Aww man, I love your gramps," Jordan announces. "Can I come for tea?"

"No, he's all mine tonight! I think we're laying down some plans for his big birthday next weekend."

I glance across at Jamie. He's still quiet but meets my smile with a smile at least.

"Are we at least invited to the party?" Jordan begs.

"You probably will be. All of you," I add, waving my arms round to encompass them all.

I realise Jamie has never met Gramps and he probably feels a bit left out so my arm waving includes him too.

Jordan turns to look at Jamie. "You'll love him, Jamie. He's the way coolest old person I have ever known."

Katie gives out a snort.

"I'll look forward to it. I feel very honoured to be asked. Thanks, Danny."

Did I just colour in the cheek department a little? Again, FFS! Nobody mentions it if I did. I get the feeling people want to ask things but it's all a bit awkward.

Hmmmm!

First bell. Jamie and I head off to maths. He is still very quiet and I'm wondering if it has to do with the text mix-up and associated replies.

"Sorry about sending you Katie's text last night." I break the ice. Something has to be said.

"Hey, don't worry," Jamie says, but I feel there is something else. Nothing is forthcoming though. Is that the end of that then? The end of what though? We walk on in silence. I feel as though I've ruined things. Jamie got really protective in school when I fell apart then I sent him a wrong text, which he could read so many ways. He is probably emotionally drained too.

"Are we ok?" I ask, stopping him before we enter the classroom. "I feel I messed up yesterday what with one thing and another. I like having you as a friend," I blurt out. "I don't want to lose that."

Jamie gives me a hug. The first hug. A manly hug. Just the right length for a straight guy? Probably! "We are very much OK, Danny. Sorry if I was a bit cool. I think I was just worried with Katie knowing about the text thing."

Why worried, I wonder? "Did she mention it?" I ask in horror.

"In passing, but all good. I just wasn't sure how you were going to react seeing us all there." He squeezed my arm. "But we are very good." He smiles a gorgeous smile. All was well in Danny World.

Maybe he just needed to be reassured I was OK with it all too.

I rush home after school. Dad had said he would be back early too; we expected Gramps at about 4.30. Maybe we were the three musketeers. Well, maybe not, but we did all rub along brilliantly. Sorry if I sound as if I have the perfect life. I really don't, but what I do have is the most perfect family unit. There's only three of us. Sadly, I never knew my grandma as she died from cancer before I was born and Gramps never remarried. He seems happy enough and has loads of activities he's always involved in and telling us about.

Dad's car is at the top of the drive and sure enough, Gramps's green Mini Clubman is there behind it.

"Here he is," beams Gramps as I enter the kitchen. I give him a big hug. "Let me look at you," he says, holding me at arm's length. "I swear you grow an inch every time I see you and you get more handsome by the day!" He laughs.

"Sure, Gramps, and your eyesight is getting worse every time you visit."

"Boys." Dad throws me a look but it's a happy look. We all know that the one link all three of us have is Mum, and she holds us together.

"So, sixth form," Gramps says. "How's it going? First week and all that."

I regale him of the first week, leaving out Jamie. I'm sure he would be fine with me being gay, but as Dad doesn't know yet, Gramps is a bit further down the line. Anyway, what am I thinking? Jamie is not gay, just a history buddy and all-round good guy.

"So, a history buddy." Gramps smiles. "That sounds like fun. Dad tells me that you're going to use some of Mum's project stuff to help you along."

"We are, yes, I'm super excited. I may even take Jamie to Holbrooke, see if we got a feeling for the project."

"Are you OK with that, Danny?" Dad asks. "I know that was your special place with Mum."

"I know, but I want to share my memories with people. I have to move on." There's an awkward silence and I realise what I have said. "I don't mean, move on as in, you know, moving on. I just don't want Holbrooke and the other places Mum and I used to go to turned into museum pieces where I never go again."

"I think you're absolutely right, Danny, and going with someone else, and maybe someone who didn't know Mum, might make it easier for you." Gramps was, as ever, very astute.

"Anyway, I haven't actually mentioned that to Jamie yet, so it may not happen."

Gramps reaches for his tea. "Oh, yes," he says, holding his cup aloft. "I hear you have a snazzy coffee machine in the common room too."

"We do, still have to pay for it so I don't bother."

"Sounds like fun. A bit different to when I was at the grammar school. We certainly didn't have a coffee machine."

"To be fair, Gramps, was there such a thing as a coffee machine back then?"

"Hey, I'm coming up seventy, not seven hundred, I'll have you know. Come to think about it though, I can remember camp coffee."

Camp coffee? That conjures up a whole new thing!

"It came in a bottle and tasted of tar."

"It makes our coffee machine sound like the best thing ever."

I look across at Gramps as he's chatting away about the good old times. He is smartly dressed in well-cut jeans, Chelsea boots, a cream shirt, and dark blue waistcoat. I hope I still have it when I'm coming up seventy. His eyes sparkle and he is looking so happy. Then I remember he lost his wife aged just forty-nine and his daughter at thirty-nine. He has so much to be angry about, to be bitter over, but he exudes happiness.

What a guy. And, he's my gramps. My heart overflows, as it always does when I see him.

"So," Dad starts, "this party."

"Now, Charlie, I don't want all this fuss."

"It's a big number, Gramps," I say. "Has to be celebrated."

He pulls a face. "Why can't we just have a little do, maybe here?"

"We could plan a barbecue but late September could be dodgy weather wise," Dad suggests.

"Just a cake and a few sandwiches will be fine. And of course, Danny's lovely friends. It's good to surround yourself with vibrant young folk."

Jordan, vibrant? Manic, more like. Katie, vibrant? Bossy cow, more like.

Ha!

"The bowls club are putting on a tea for me too." Gramps pulls a face.

"You'll love it, Gramps."

"I know I will but it doesn't hurt to keep them on their toes." He chuckles.

"You can be a one."

"I hope so. Still got it."

"Always will have!" I fist bump him.

So, a cake, some sandwiches, some young people. It sounds so Gramps.

"Did I tell you about Mavis and the parrot?" he starts.

Probably not for these pages!

I'm laid on my bed. One happy boy. I'm always on a high after a Gramps visit and he's been on form. I think he's looking forward to his birthday and he loves it when people think he's not seventy. I remember on the bus once, only last year, and the driver thought he was using someone else's pass. Gramps loved it.

My phone pings.

Katie

How was Gramps?

Me

Top form

Brilliant night

Buzzing

Katie

Hope you gave him my love

Me

Always do my sweet.

Katie

Aaaw.

And the other thing?

Me

What other thing?

Katie

Jamie!

I forgot I hadn't really seen her on her own today.

Me

We're good.

Katie

He seemed weird today.

Qjuiet?

Me

He's fine and you don't spell quiet with a j!

Katie

Smart Alec.

My phone pings.

Jamie

You're gonna hate me.

Me to Katie

Jamie's texting. Can I catch you in abit, don't want the same as….

Katie

Ok, no problem and just for the record there's a space between 'a' and 'bit' lol!

Me to Jamie

Don't think so

What's up?

Jamie

Told Mum about us doing project work tomorrow

Me

Yep?

Jamie

She said we are looking at sofas!

Me

Sofas!

That's a new excuse

Jamie

Danny, I'm so sorry.

Me

It's fine.

It's not fine.

It's really not fine.

It was going to be the icing on my lovely life.

Jamie

I told her I didn't need to be there

She said as I would be sitting on it more than her, I needed to pick it

Me

Wow!

Jamie

Precisely

I'm gutted

Me

We'll just do another day

But deep down, I am gutted.

Jamie

I'll make it up to you

Wonder what he has in mind.

I smiled at possible scenarios.

Stop. It. Now!

Me

Bring doughnuts

Sure way to make me smile

Jamie

You're on

Was just hoping we would get a head start before Monday class

Me

I'll have a look at Mum's stuff tomorrow

Jamie

Ok

Can't wait to have a look at your mum's stuff

Is that ok to say?

Me

Sure

Jamie

Don't want to overstep the mark

Me

It's the new me with your help

Jamie

Sorry?

Me

Time I was happy when Mum is mentioned

Smiley time

No more tears

Jamie

Ok

So long as you know it's still ok for a few tears

Now and again

Me

Will do

I have been so looking forward to doing project work with Jamie that when we realise, looking at each other's commitments for next week, that we wouldn't be able to get together until Saturday after all, I'm feeling down.

What is wrong with me?

Chill, FFS!

I just love being around him.

Me

So enjoy sofas tomorrow

Jamie

Don't remind me.

Mum has other things lined up for us to do too

While we are out, we might as well just ... she says

Me

Make sure you get a big squidgy one with lots of fat cushions.

Too gay?

Jamie

Don't worry, I will. It's gonna cost her!

Me

Better go down.

Film night Friday with Dad

Jamie

That's so cool

What cha watching?

Me

Dad's choice tonight. Don't know.

Jamie

Enjoy

I'll let you know which sofa we get

Pictures too

Me

Can't wait

Later

Jamie

Night

He's so easy to talk to. A bit like a male version of Katie. I've only known him a week; less than that, in fact.

I give a big sigh. So much easier being straight. Just walk up to a girl, tell her you fancy her, it can go one of two ways. Go up to a guy and tell him you fancy him, that could lead to a punch in the face and everyone knowing you're gay.

I don't want to be straight, by the way. Just for the record.

Dad shouts up to say there's Monster Munch and gummi teeth. That means it's a horror film.

"Found this for us on Amazon," he says. The screen is frozen at the titles. 'The Cannibals and the Carpet Fitters'.

I open my eyes wide. "Sounds... Intriguing... Different!"

"Lots of killings."

I imagine the carpet fitters are not going to do well here.

Just for the record, they didn't, but if you like hammy horrors with loads of blood, then go check it out.

CHAPTER 7

BEING GAY

As it's the end of the week, and quite an eventful one, maybe it's time to fill you in a bit on how I came to be gay.

Well, maybe that's not quite right. I didn't 'come to be gay.' I didn't choose to be gay. I didn't wake up one morning and think, *Let's be gay this week.*

It was in the middle term of last year and in drama we were doing this workshop called 'Comfort Zone' when it all started. Maybe looking back after the events of that day, it started before then but I hadn't realised. Still just sixteen, young and innocent.

But I digress.

We were sat around on the bean bags in the drama studio. Mrs Evans, heavily pregnant, was perched on a stool and telling us we all had to jump outside our comfort zone sometimes, and do stuff we didn't enjoy. She wanted us to experiment with some things we might not normally want to do and the first one was kissing.

Not sure how I felt about that. I could probably kiss Mel, I thought. In the name of drama!

Lots of 'oohs' and someone shouted out, "Lee Black, this is

up your street."

"Hardly out of his comfort zone, Miss!" called another.

"But what if it's someone you really don't want to kiss or have no feelings for?"

A thought ran through my mind. Why would you even kiss someone if you didn't want to? What would be the point in that and what would be the purpose?

Lee Black would probably snog the face off a golden retriever. I could see he would be asked to sit this one out.

Instead, I found my name being called out. I wasn't particularly bothered and glanced across at Mel, who was animated, chatting to her neighbour. I was happy to immerse myself in some role play. I knew that's all it was. Who was my chosen subject?

Marc Laconza.

I did a double take.

"Eeew, a gay kiss?" Lee Black piped up.

"You're next," someone called out.

Ha blooming ha!

Marc walked out to the front. We both looked awkward.

"Now I'm not forcing anyone to do anything they don't want to so I will ask if you're both happy."

We looked at each other. Marc said he was happy to if I was. It was only acting, after all. I shrugged and agreed. My heart was pounding.

Why?

"OK." Mrs Evans shifted her bulk and placed a hand under her belly. "What I would like is not a peck on the cheek, but imagine you have wanted to kiss each other for like, a long time but been too afraid to but things have come to a head…"

Is this even legal?

Asking two boys to kiss in school in front of a class of impressionable sixteen-year-olds?

A guffaw from the back!

"...So, make it special."

"Can we video it?" some smart-arse shouted.

"Absolutely not. I do not want anything ending up on TikTok."

"Aaaw!"

I was starting to panic a bit. Marc was saying something to Mrs Evans.

"Hush down." She waved her arms. "Marc was asking if I wanted any dialogue. I hadn't considered it. What do you both think?" She looked at us with what seemed like hope in her eyes.

Marc was saying, "I just thought a bit of a build-up, you know."

Did Marc really want this? *What's his game?* I thought.

"Sure," I found myself saying. "Why not?"

Applause.

Really?

We hadn't done anything yet.

Then it was, "OK, go," from Mrs Evans and we were on.

I was usually quite good at improvising so thought, *Just chill and do this, Danny!*

Concentrate.

While I was still getting my head around how to approach this, Marc took my hand in his and looked me in the eyes.

Wow. I felt a spark shoot up my arm; his touch was like an

electric shock. I wasn't expecting that. Was I? Was he feeling this too? What exactly was it I was feeling?

"So, Danny, you know I've so wanted to do this for like, ages." His thumb rubbed the back of my hand and I felt the breath being sucked out of my body. *Jeez, what's happening?*

"I, er, I had no idea," I came back with. I was struggling a bit with this. Not in an 'I can't do this' sort of way, but an 'I have no idea what to say next' way.

I don't know why but I reached up and touched the side of his face. His expression was hard to read. I dropped my hand and was about to mouth, 'Sorry.'

"Good! Good!" said Mrs Evans, now on her feet.

"You are so fanciable; I'm sorry I never told you before. I wasn't sure how you would react," he continued. "I love the way your hair sort of, you know." He reached up and ruffled my hair.

Does it?

What does it sort of do?

For some reason I didn't mind him messing up my hair. It takes me ages to get it just the right way every morning; normally I'd run a mile if anyone went to touch it but I wanted him to do it again, run his hand through my hair, and down the back of my neck.

Did I almost utter a soft groan?

I wanted to pull him into an embrace.

Shit!

I then found myself asking, "Do you want to kiss me?"

Where is this coming from?

He gave a big grin and said, "I thought you'd never ask. I've been plucking up the courage."

"Plucking?" someone shouted.

As you can see, it was quite an inventive drama group!

"Quiet at the back," shouted Mrs Evans.

I think this is turning her on.

No!

We looked deep into each other's eyes and he put his hand behind my head and our lips touched gently. Heat radiated across the back of my head, down my neck, into my tummy; my heart was beating, my chest seemed to be heaving. *Is it?*

Holy shit!

What is happening?

Something is stirring!

Why?

He pulled back. "Was it OK?" he asked.

OK?

Oh-kay?

Fuck!

What's going on?

I feel like I can't speak.

Pull it back together.

People are watching.

I put my hand through his hair and smile. "We can do better than that." I pulled him back in and we went for it, full throttle. Our mouths locked and I could taste mint; his tongue touched my lips, my legs were wobbling, his hand was on my face, my hand was back in his hair. Where was this going?

The class was quiet. I thought there would be catcalls, but nothing.

I didn't want this to end. What was wrong with me? Was there something wrong with me? I felt like I could hear soft music. I could feel the sun on my back, I heard birds, felt butterflies tumbling in my tummy. Everything felt warm, sugar coated; I had no worries at all, this just felt so freaking awesome.

Marc pulled back.

No!

'Don't stop!' I wanted to shout at him. I still had my hand in his hair. Reluctantly I pulled it away and gave him a smile. He smiled back.

"Wow," said Mrs Evans.

"Are you two actually gay?" someone shouted.

I coloured slightly.

Marc gave them the finger.

I'm thinking someone might have hit a nail on its head with a hammer!

We were still close to each other and he whispered, "Was that, like, OK?"

I wanted to tell him it was the best thing that had ever happened to me. I wanted to tell him to kiss me again. I wanted to hold him in my arms. I wanted… "Sure, just a drama class. I think we got it in the bag."

We went back to our places.

Mel said, "Good job."

Someone else said "That was amazing." Then, "Did you rehearse that?"

I just smiled back because I feared if I opened my mouth to say anything I would blurt something out or spout an absolute load of crap.

Katie was across the room staring at me like she'd just had a lightbulb moment. I smiled at her. Her eyes were wide and she mouthed, 'Oh my god.'

Later as Katie and I walked home she broached the subject.

"So," she started, "you seemed to enjoy that kiss."

What could I tell her? "Did I?"

She linked her arm in mine and we continued walking. "Didn't you?"

I was quiet for a moment until she looks at me questioningly. "I cannot lie. I felt something."

"Stirring down below?"

I look at her in horror. How did she know all this stuff? "How did you know?"

"Well, either you took lessons from Bradley Cooper beforehand or it just felt," she faltered, 'right.'

I was quiet.

"It was so convincing. The whole class was quiet. That never happens."

"What does it mean?" I asked.

"You think I'm asking if you're gay?"

"Is that not what's happening here?"

"Not if that's not what you're feeling."

"Could I be gay?" I stopped and looked at her. "I've kissed a girl before and…"

"Who? When?"

"Never mind." I needed to say this. "I've kissed a girl and it felt, well, sort of yuck. All sloppy and cold and I couldn't wait for it to be over."

I was quiet and so was Katie. I think she knew better than to break into my 'coming out', if indeed that's what was about to happen.

I continued. "I was happy to do the kiss today. It was only drama, it's all an act, after all, but...' I paused again. Not for dramatic effect this time. "But it felt so different to kissing a girl. It was warm and passionate. I thought I was going to fall over, the charge that went through me. The touch of his hand was like an electric shock, then we kissed again more passionately and, and, and, I didn't want it to stop. I know we were only acting. I know he was acting. I know he'd be thinking 'job done, that went well, brownie points,' and will have moved on, but OMG, I certainly didn't think we were acting by the end. It felt so real. if that means I'm gay then, then..."

"Bring it on?" Katie asked, squeezing my arm.

I knew Katie would know when she saw the kiss that it was more than acting, certainly for me anyway.

"I don't know. I wasn't expecting to find out I was gay when I came into school this morning."

"It all makes sense now," Katie continued, linking my arm and dragging me along again.

"Whoa, wait, what do you mean?" I asked.

"Just little things recently. Seen you looking."

Had I been?

Who at?

Boys?

"You made a comment about some guy's trainers."

"Really?" I asked, trying to remember.

"You said they looked lush. I think it was Billy Mackenzie."

Again, I said, "Really?"

"Yep." I think Katie was silently pleased she had known before me. "And you commented on Ali's hair, and I'm sure you were looking at his arse the other—"

"Stop," I said, feeling slightly horrified. "Do other people think the same? Has anyone said anything? Shit, have I been inappropriate?"

"Not in the slightest. You were being honest and I think it's so cool. You and Marc would be so cute together."

I pulled Katie to another stop. "OK, now we are going to stop talking about this. Yes, that kiss was awesome but..."

"But what?" Katie asked.

"Wow."

"Too gay for your own good."

Shit.

Gay?

Me?

Yep!

Get over it!

And that was how it all came out. I came out to Katie. I knew I was gay after that kiss.

Marc, I'm sure didn't feel the same way. He never mentioned it and certainly didn't follow up on it. I didn't mind. Not really. Well, maybe a little bit, but hey, I've moved on. I have a new project, quite literally, with my history buddy.

CHAPTER 8

Monday 25th September

I'm still checking myself in the mirror. Knowing I will be sitting next to Jamie again this morning in history, I need to make sure this hair goes that way and that one the other way. Maybe I should have it like him, all chopped off!

Well, maybe not.

I've paired up a plain white tee-shirt with black jeans, simple. Jamie will walk in looking as though he's just thrown some old stuff on and will look amazing.

I'm chatting to Jordan in the common room when Jamie walks in looking as though he's just thrown some old stuff on and looks amazing.

I kid you not.

"Hey, guys. Good weekend?" he asks.

"Hey, Jamie." Jordan pats him on the back. "Not bad at all, went to see that new film on Saturday."

"Danny was watching a good film the other night." Jamie nods in my direction.

"Really?" Jordan raises his eyebrows. "You didn't say."

"It was just film night, some hammy horror my dad chose."

"I like your dad's choice of films. When I've stayed over, we watched some amazing stuff."

"Yeah, stuff we shouldn't have watched at times."

Jamie puts his hands on his hips. "Not porn, I hope."

I colour and instantly deny any porn was watched.

Jamie grins at me.

Stop!

"Ready for project DaJa?"

"Project who?" Jordan asks.

"We were going to call it JaDa but that's someone connected with Will Smith, then DanJam but that sounded too weird," I say.

"Whoa, what jam?" Jordan rubs his face. "That's conjuring up all sorts of stuff and not in a good way. I'll stick with DaJa. But what does it mean?"

"Just this history project," Jamie explains. "First two letters of each of our names. We had to give it a name."

"Should have called it Capability Ross," Jordan says.

"What do you know about landscape gardening?" I ask, surprised he would have heard of Capability Brown.

"Er, it was, it was your mum who told me about him years back and the name just stuck in this old head of mine." He bashed the side of his head.

"Glad you remembered something she told you." I laugh.

Jamie sort of purses his lips and nods, which I think means, 'Nice one. You did that without getting emotional.'

Which, by the way, I'm pleased with.

Today is a day of two halves. The morning flies by, as I

imagined it would, sitting next to a gorgeous boy and feeling his heat radiate across me as we crack on with our project. We manage to do a lot of good stuff and line up some to do on Saturday. I'm on a high when we meet with Katie, Sam, and Jordan for lunch.

I was to be brought down to earth in English.

We have a new teacher, Miss Waycross, who is filling in for Mrs Evans; she is now the proud owner of a small person and is on maternity leave. I have to say, I am really missing her. Miss Waycross is older, maybe forty, and a bit cold, I feel. Katie and Jordan aren't in this English set. I miss having Katie in English. I am sat next to Jen as Miss has seated us alphabetically so she could get to know our names. I don't usually hang with Jen and she seems a bit off, not being able to sit with who she's used to. But we rub along OK.

"Have you read any of this?" Jen asks, holding up her copy of *The Little Bluebird*.

I want to say, 'Well obviously, as that's what we were told to do,' but I just say, "Sure, found it a bit depressing actually."

"I thought it was crap," Jen says, implying by the word 'was', that she in fact read it all. "There's no substance to the story," she adds, tapping the cover with an immaculately polished nail.

"So," starts Miss Waycross, "anyone got anything to say about the initial feel of the book?"

"There's no substance to the story," Jen says. Way to go, Jen, tell it like it is.

"But don't you think you have to dig deeper and imagine the underlying feelings of the narrator?" Miss is wandering down the aisle towards her.

"Not at all," Jen carries on. "The narrator is too bland to even think he has other feelings."

"There is a passage in chapter three that makes you feel there is more to the narrator than it seems." This from Jack, sat by the window.

"I agree, Jack. Perhaps Daniel would like to read that passage out and we can see if we can change Jen's obvious distaste."

There is silence.

"Who is Daniel?" asks Raheem sat at the front.

Miss Waycross swivels to face me. She has grasped a few names in the week she has been with us.

"Are you not Daniel?" she asks.

Before I can speak, Raheem adds to his question. "No-one calls him Daniel. I thought we had a new student."

Someone sniggers.

"OK, settle down." Miss Waycross is looking at me. "Daniel?"

"Everyone calls me Danny, Miss," I say.

Maybe should have just read the damn passage.

"It says Daniel in the register. If that is your given name then I can call you that."

"Well, my given name is Jennifer, Miss, but you call me Jen!" Jen sprung to my defence. "And Tony..." she starts, looking at Tony, who is actually Antony.

"Enough," Miss Waycross says. "Does your mother not call you Daniel? Such a lovely name."

There is total silence.

You could hear a pin drop.

On a piece of felt.

"His mother was killed in a horrific car accident," Raheem again. "So..." He trails off, realising maybe the use of the word 'horrific' was slightly over the top, although he's pretty much correct. He shuts up.

My eyes prick.

Here we go.

Some things are always going to set me off.

"I'm sorry," Miss Waycross says. "Was it recently?"

"Year 9," says someone. Everyone knows, everyone remembers.

"But that's two years ago. Are you not over it yet?"

What?

What. The. Absolute. Fuck?

I realise I'm breathing deeply. My hands are balled into fists. If I say one word here, I will be expelled so I quietly stand up, put my book in my bag and walk out.

"Where are you going?" She follows me to the door. "Get back in here."

"I can't talk to you now," I say, walking down the corridor.

"Headmaster's office on your way."

"Happy to!" I shout. "If anything happened to you, would you want your family just to forget you?"

I turn and run.

"No running!"

FUCK OFF.

I WILL NOT ever forget my mum and nobody will make me do so. I can move on, do stuff to make me happy, which is what Dad and me do. Gramps, too, and all my friends. I don't sit in my bedroom all day crying. Some days I could, but I don't. I'm trying to be strong. I really am. I really don't need a total stranger telling me to 'get over it.'

I really don't.

I turn the corridor and run headlong into Mr Brownlow; he had been my form tutor last year.

"Whoa," he says, rescuing me from falling. "OK?"

"Sorry, Sir, I, er, I…" He sees my tears.

More bloody tears.

I really need to man up.

Deal with this in a different way.

"Come on." He leads me into an empty classroom and sits me down, pulling up a chair opposite me. "Just breathe a moment." He can see my distress.

This is so stupid.

I can't be like this in a meeting in five years when someone mentions my mum.

"Want to tell me about it?"

Mr Brownlow had had to deal with me and my fallout when Mum died so he knew all there was to about the events.

"It's totally stupid, Sir. I just overreacted to a comment. Instead of handling it differently, I just sat there in silence and someone else said something about, you know, about Mum and, well, you know."

I realise I am shaking.

Mr Brownlow takes my hands in his large, protective, comforting grasp.

I'm blinking furiously to stop any further tears.

"It won't go away, Danny. It's good that you remember and you will get upset. Nobody said anything that needs reporting?"

No, just get rid of that cow who teaches English and has no feelings. Just like the narrator of that stupid bloody book. That's what I want to say but don't.

"No, Sir, she didn't know."

"Who?"

"Miss Waycross."

"Oh?"

"Just a misunderstanding and I walked out. I didn't deal with it well."

"Do you want me to have a word? Explain to her? Maybe the three of us sit down together?"

He releases my hands but they are still shaking slightly.

"I just feel she is, well, she is very cold. She said, she actually said that I, that I should be, well I should be over it by now."

"Christ," Mr Brownlow says. "Sorry, probably shouldn't have said that."

"It's OK, Sir, I won't say anything."

"Let me have a word and maybe suggest we meet together."

I sigh. "Why can't I handle this better, Sir?"

"We all deal with stuff in our own way, Danny. I know kids who would probably throw a party if anything happened to their mum or dad, but you're different. You had a great thing going with your mum. I met her many times and you and her just had this amazing bond. There is nothing to be sorry for about getting emotional or feeling protective towards her." He takes my shaking hands in his and squeezes them in a fatherly way. "Don't ever change, Danny Ross. You are one of the good guys, someone who will make a difference in life and because you feel the way you do, this will help you as you grow older, to understand many, many things."

Mr Brownlow is a very wise bird.

If I had to choose a second dad, I'd choose Mr Brownlow.

I look up at him and smile. "Thanks, Sir, you always made me feel better about it."

He releases my hands and glances up at the clock. "Don't go back to class, Danny. Go and get a coffee in the common room."

A coffee?

Going back to class would be less scary, but I'm not going back to class.

"OK, Sir. I'm glad it was you I bumped into."

"So am I, Danny. I'll sort it."

I'm sat by the window in the common room trying to read a book, when in fact I am staring out of the window down onto the picnic tables below. There are three boys larking about on one of them. One is stood on the bench doing some moves; they are probably twelve. Maybe I wish I was twelve again. Mum would still have been here, I wouldn't know I was gay, just messing about with Jordan, having fun, going home to Mum and Dad. Tears prick my eyes yet again. Why can I not turn this off!

Katie flies in after the bell has sounded.

"Oh my god, are you OK?"

"Yes, I'm fine." I look up. The jungle drums haven't taken long then. I realise Sam is in my English class. She will have texted Katie, like, before I was down the corridor!

"How could she? Who does she think she is?"

"Calm down. I overreacted."

"But you walked out."

"I know, and I shouldn't have. I should have been quicker off the mark or just…" I trail off.

"You don't have to, Danny." Katie is furious.

"Stop." I held my hands up. "Really, it's not worth it."

"Has she got kids? Would she like it if—"

"Please, Katie, stop. I'm cool. I've calmed down. I shouldn't have let her get to me."

"But…"

"I'm leaving if you don't stop."

Katie is blinking furiously. I normally let her rant and get it out of her system.

"I need to take a better handle on this, Katie," I say, pulling her down into the next seat. "I can't go off on one every time." I nearly mention Jamie and his advice but this will probably wind her up to the next level so I keep quiet.

Jen comes over next, followed by Raheem; Raheem, of all people. I actually feel for him. He is distraught about what he said.

"Man, I'm so sorry, it just sort of came out, and, you know I didn't mean it in a, well, in that way?" He is so flustered.

"I know, bud, you don't have to apologise. You were mad, as were a lot of people, and I'm so grateful that you all stick up for me." I jump up and give him a hug. "We're good," I add.

This is exactly why I need to handle things better because all this sympathy and arm stroking only makes me worse. I put up with it because I know people mean well and I need them to still be there for me but I can't wait to get out.

Jamie hasn't appeared and maybe that is a good thing. I don't want to break down again in front of him. It may wear him down and I don't want to lose his friendship. I have already decided not to mention it if he doesn't.

And...

I'm going to be stronger from this moment on.

So, laid on my bed that night I reflect on the highs and lows of Monday and decide I need to focus on the highs and forget the lows.

"Mum," I start, "I need you to know I always loved you and I always will but I need to keep you in my heart and not my tears from now on. It doesn't help with others to see me crying all the time. Strange as it may sound, maybe Miss Waycross was a little bit right when she asked if I'd not gotten over it. Bad choice of words, maybe, and had she said things in a nicer way then I wouldn't have reacted as I did.'

"Who are you talking to?" Dad asks, passing my door.

"Just Mum."

"OK."

No more needs to be said.

No texts from Jamie tonight, and I don't feel like texting him. I'm worried he may have heard but doesn't want to mention it because he's afraid of me melting down again. Maybe he hasn't heard.

That's fine.

I did text Katie and Jordan and say I didn't want to rake it up tomorrow so asked them not to mention it.

They both agreed.

I feel a bit flat.

What I probably could do with is a big hug from Jamie.

Don't think that's going to happen.

CHAPTER 9
Friday 29th September

The gang are all at the benches the next morning as well as Sam, Tony, and Raheem.

I know before I get there that Katie has said something to them all because the unbelievable noisy chatter and false laughter is, well, false. However, I'm happy with that so I sneak in next to Katie and she hugs me tight. "Morning, honey. How are you?"

I hug her back and put my head on her shoulder. "I'm grand, thanks."

Jamie sits opposite and seems to just stare at us. Weird?

He shoots a question about football to Jordan and they carry on chatting about it.

I whisper to Katie, "Is Jamie… OK?"

"Think so, why?"

"He hasn't spoken to me."

"Don't be paranoid."

"OK," I whisper back.

But, come the afternoon and maths I can sense an atmosphere is still hanging awkwardly. He's always so carefree and chatty.

Nothing.

I take my seat next to him. "Sorry I didn't get to chat this morning. You and Jordan seemed engrossed in football talk," I venture. "Never did understand the beautiful game."

"That's OK."

I wait.

Was that it?

I turn to face front, thinking about what to say, if anything. As usual my paranoia is rising up, wondering what it is I said or did, or is he pissed because I never told him about yesterday?

What can I say to make it right? Just tell him? Moaning again isn't going to help us.

Jamie beats me to it.

"I thought you might have said something about what happened in English."

Yikes, are we married already?

"Sorry, I just thought after all the grief I had put you through, and you had kinda rescued me once already, I didn't want to be in a flood of tears again in front of you. Also, on reflection I could have handled it a lot better so I was, correction am, feeling a bit stupid. I let Mum get in the way again."

"Yeah, well," he says.

Yeah, well? What does that mean?

I look across at his face and can't quite read him this morning. "You're not really..." And I pause, not having given enough thought to what I was going to say.

"Not what? Pissed off? Feeling left out of the loop?" Jamie continues to stare ahead.

Oh, crikey, I had really cocked up. Why hadn't I just texted him and told him about yesterday? Maybe that was childish of me. Is this the end of something special? This is the second time he has been weird; maybe this is his way? Would I be better off without him in my life? Don't need a moody guy, and I certainly don't need a jealous guy.

Jordan bounces into my head, screaming 'Roxy Music!'

"I'm really sorry," I say. "I just didn't think." I end it there, not wanting to moan and gripe on again.

"No, you didn't."

There's what seems like an eternal pause.

"Bollocks," I say. "I'm so crap at this. I cock everything up that is good in my life. I should have told you. I wish I had. Please don't hate me."

Why do I say that? Do I think this is where this is going? Should I move? No more history buddy? No more being his guru?

There's another pause then out of the corner of eye do I see his shoulders sag.

"I should be the one saying sorry." He turns to face me. "Your life has had so much shit in it. I'm sorry, Danny."

"Whatever for?"

"Being a mardy bastard."

"You were a bit quiet, but that's all."

"I wasn't just quiet. I was shooting you down and you don't deserve that after what happened yesterday. I should be here to support you."

"You are always supporting me. I guess I thought you might be getting a bit sick of doing it. I'm such a flake."

"No, you're not."

"I feel it at times. I'm really trying to turn it round."

Jamie goes quiet again.

"OK?" I ask him.

"I had a big row with Mum last night, so that just added to how I was feeling at the time."

"Oh, shit, sorry."

"She came in from work in a bad mood and things just, well... sort of exploded. Every time we have a row Dad's name is brought up and she's off on one."

I'm not sure if I should be asking if he wants to talk about it.

"Then I look at the bigger picture," he concludes.

Now I don't really know what he means.

He looks at me. "I bet... what you wouldn't give to have a huge row with your mum, just to get to talk to her. Here I am moaning on about..." Jamie trails off and hangs his head.

Wow, that was unexpected.

"And then I'm off with you just because I thought you should have told me." He swung round to face me. "I totally get why you didn't want to talk to anyone about it. I can't believe your teacher said what she did."

"I think Mr Brownlow is going to have a word with her. Just to explain the situation. But now I've slept on it I'd rather he didn't. I don't want any unwanted atmosphere with Miss Waycross. I need good grades in English and not a teacher who thinks I like to think I'm clever."

"Maybe he's already said something?"

"More than likely." I look him in the eye worriedly. "Bollocks," I say.

Jamie smiles. "Exactly."

ORDINARY BOY

"Maybe I'll seek her out and apologise before she says anything. Don't want anything else said in class."

Jamie is quiet again.

"Are we OK though? I'd hate for us to fall out. I should really have at least mentioned it."

"We are fine." He does that 'squeezing my shoulder' thing, which seems to be his trademark 'life is OK' thing.

Which I quite like.

Miss Wilson makes an entrance and it's faces forward again.

At break I head off to the staff room intent on making my peace with Miss Waycross. Have to say, I'm not relishing the thought. It could blow up in my face if she's still mad at me, which to be fair, if it was me, I would be.

A teacher I don't know opens the door and smiles nicely. Obviously hasn't been here long. She heads off to find Miss Waycross and a moment later she comes to the door.

"Daniel," she says.

I instantly think we still have issues.

But.

Then.

"Sorry, Danny."

"I'm sorry, Miss. I want to apologise for my behaviour yesterday," I start. I fiddle with the strap of my rucksack. "I need to really get to grips with my... er, my..."

She steps out of the doorway and closes it and we move near the window on the corridor. "You have nothing to get to grips with, Danny. I actually gave myself a talking to last night. I have never had to suffer loss like you have and I should have instantly sorted it out, and I certainly should not have said what I did." If she had a rucksack, she would be fiddling with the strap right now.

"But that doesn't make my outburst acceptable and for that I am sorry." I look her in the face. "I've never ever walked out of a lesson before and I feel pretty crap about it."

"Well, that's very mature of you, Danny. I'm sorry I made a big deal about the name thing. As someone correctly pointed out to me, there are at least five other people who have shortened names and they are all called by them."

"I don't want us to have problems. I work hard and…" I start.

"From what I've seen and heard you are one of the better students, Danny. Mr Brownlow was very clear about that." Miss Waycross smiles then adds, "I'm sure I shouldn't actually say that to you, though."

"I didn't ask him to say anything. I wish he hadn't."

"He did what was right, Danny. He wouldn't have been doing his job otherwise. How about we have a fresh start in the next lesson, pretend we are meeting for the first time? And I am so sorry about your mum, and even though I can't imagine what you went through I, as your English teacher, will always be there if you need to talk about anything."

She actually reaches across and squeezes my shoulder!

Two shoulder squeezes in one morning.

The day is improving.

Do I need to sort anything out with anyone else?

No, all good, thanks!

Jordan skuttles up to me outside the gates later and puts his arm across my shoulder. "Just remind me," he says, "what is it I'm not supposed to be telling people?"

"What do you mean?"

"Katie said something this morning and I was only half listening."

"Half listening? That's good for you, before school has even started."

"Sixth form," he corrects me. "Haven't waited sixteen years to still be at school."

Sometimes I wonder if he wasn't left behind in year nine!

"It was to do with, well, it doesn't matter now because it's all sorted."

"But what if someone asks me something about this thing that I don't know anything about and I say the wrong thing?" He seems genuinely concerned.

"Jordan, buddy, if you can't remember what it was about, how will you say the wrong thing about it?"

He stands up straight. "True. You have a valid point there."

We walk on a bit.

"So, it wasn't to do with you and Jamie?"

"Like what? What to do with me and Jamie?"

"Katie says everything is about you and Jamie! She's desperate to get you two tog..." He falters. "Shit."

"What exactly has Katie been saying?" I ask.

"She mentioned something about you and Jamie." Jordan furrows his brow as if trying to retrieve the information from some sealed filing cabinet drawer in his head. "I think she also said not to say anything to you until you tell me about it."

"I will have to have a word or seven with Katie. If she ruins it, well, not ruins it, because there's nothing to ruin.

He's not gay," I hiss but a quiet hiss.

"Do you know he isn't?" Jordan leans in and whispers. "Katie says she's seen him looking."

Someone else looking?

Looking?

Looking at what?

Me?

Really?

When?

"Where is she?"

"Needlework or something."

"Eh? Katie doesn't do needlework."

"Hockey then?"

"That's nothing like needlework."

"It's a girl thing, I wasn't listening."

Right!

I text her.

I wait.

I'm home doing homework when she texts back.

Katie

Hey?

Me

Where are you?

Katie

Just finished Puzzler Class.

Where, where on earth did Jordan get needlework or hockey from?

Me

Right

Katie

Problem?

Me

Not sure. Jordan says you have seen Jamie looking at me.

Katie

Really!

I mean really?

Me

You didn't?

Katie

Which?

Told Jordan or saw Jamie?

Me

Everyone is talking in riddles today.

Katie

Can I come round?

Me

Sure.

Katie

Give me ten x

I knew it would be twenty minutes, not ten, and it was.

Katie lets herself in, as she always does.

I would like to say she looks gorgeous in skintight jeans, a pink hoodie, and white and pink trainers, but being gay, I don't notice. Well, not as much as I should.

I could tell you every detail of Jamie's outfit today!

No?

OK!

"So, what's up?" Katie throws herself on the sofa and looks across at me.

"I don't know. I had a thing where Jamie wasn't talking to me. I really thought I'd blown it, then he was talking to me, then I had a surreal conversation with Miss Waycross who has gone from evil witch to girl next door baking apple pie, to Jordan saying you were at needlework and had seen Jamie giving me the eye. My head is proper hurting today!"

"Did I say that to Jordan?"

I shrug and hold my hands out, asking the question.

"Wait, Jordan asked me what the craic was between you and Jamie and I said as far as I knew there wasn't any, then..." She sits up and pauses.

"Then?" I prompt her.

"No, I definitely didn't say I had seen him looking."

She lays back down. "You know what Jordan is like."

Sadly, I do but that's why I love him.

"So, nothing new on that front?" she asks.

I fill her in on the maths frosty start and the full Miss Waycross story.

"Good job I hadn't been in that class. I'd have pulped her!"

"That's what I would have been worried about. I think Jamie would have done the same. You're all so protective of me."

"We need to look after you."

Jamie doesn't love me.

Katie isn't looking for love.

Jordan is looking for love.

Who will be the first to reap any rewards?

I have a deep gut feeling that if Jordan cuts his hair, it could well be him.

Remember back at the start I was helping Dad get ready for his date? Well, here we are again – Groundhog Day! The good thing is, he has remembered the tips – right shirt, different belt, you know the things.

"So," I start, "still feeling anxious or did the last date help?"

"Why am I doing this?"

"You don't have to, you know. You can text and say… say I'm ill or something."

"Don't tempt fate. It'll be fine."

"Sure?"

"Yep, sure. What's the worst that can happen?"

My eyes widen, imagining a chainsaw, a manic grin and lots of blood. "It'll be fine. Like you say. You're meeting in a public place, aren't you?"

"Nando's."

"Then that's grand. Nothing to worry about." And… I am so not going to pace about the kitchen cleaning cupboards waiting for him to get back like last time.

At ten thirty, I am just putting crockery back in a cupboard I have cleaned.

I kid you not!

I didn't even think I was doing it until I noticed stuff all over the kitchen.

I hear the front door open and close.

Deep intake of breath.

"So?"

"Yeah." Dad shrugs off his jacket and puts it on the back of the chair. No tossing it on the sofa.

He doesn't head for wine either.

OK, good signs.

"Sarah was very nice."

"OK."

Give me more.

"She's an author. Writing a book."

Hm, could have worked that out.

"Anything we've heard of?"

"Think it's factual, so probably not."

"So, she was nice?" I hate that word.

"I think we hit it off OK. We exchanged numbers."

Wow. Serious stuff.

"Seeing her again then?"

"Hope so, we've left it open for now."

Maybe not so serious then.

"She has a lot on. I think she does some proofreading and other stuff too. Tutoring, too, I think."

"Don't force it if you don't want to," I say. "You'll know if it's right."

"Thanks, Dr Freud. Maybe I should hook you up with Sarah, you could bounce ideas off each other."

Ha! Right!

I sort of worried for Dad and then again, I didn't. I would love him to find someone special. I know deep down Mum is the only one for him, and even though she's not around he still feels closely linked to her. I also know he would worry about me, even though I'm sure I would be totally fine because that's the type of person I am. I could not be the nightmare stepson throwing crockery at the wall. It would take far too much effort. And I've just cleaned it all for goodness' sake!

Maybe Dad and I are destined to have a cool dad/son life. Doing stuff together, hanging out. Sometimes he's more like an older brother to me as we can talk about anything without getting freaked out. But there is the companionship side of things and we could probably both do with that.

At some point.

Maybe not today.

But at some point.

Time for bed!

Tomorrow is history project day. At my house. Just me and Jamie. I'm feeling a bit flat, if truth be told. I've now convinced myself it's just 'mates', and I would be cool with that because at least we got to hang out, and he was good to hang out with. I was hoping to find out a bit more about him and his previous life, as I would have him to myself.

I can still dream. Dreams are cheap.

Did I say that before?

CHAPTER 10

Saturday 30th September

Morning

Sun streaming through the crack in the curtains. Dad running a shower.

I roll over and check my phone. No messages. A good sign. For some reason I felt there would be a message from Jamie saying he was unable to come. I can't explain why. Well, yes I can, it's the paranoia!

I feel almost trance-like.

I shower. We have two, just to be clear. Dad wasn't running a shower for me.

I head downstairs. Dad is there already, wet hair plastered down.

"Morning," he says cheerfully, giving me a big smile.

"For what reason is this mega amount of happiness shining from you?" I ask.

"No reason. Sun is shining. It's Saturday. Off to the rugby with Carl; life is good."

"Excellent."

He looks at me. "You seem a bit... spaced? Is that the right word? Vague?"

"Just feel a bit off."

"Thought you'd be looking forward to Jamie calling."

"I am. Maybe it's the whole project thing and thinking about Mum."

I was supposed to be trying to stop all this.

"Just think, she would absolutely love you to firstly be doing a project on what she knew so much about, and secondly she'd be thrilled to think her hard work was being used to help you both."

"You're right. Got to try to shake off this feeling."

"Good lad." Dad is wiping surfaces down.

"I can do that if you want to get away," I offer.

"No panic. What time are you expecting Jamie?"

"About ten thirty." I look up at the clock which tells me it is 09:55am.

"I'll be gone by then. I'll have to meet him another time."

"Sure."

Dad ruffles my already ruffled but gelled into place hair as he walks past on his way back upstairs.

"Thanks, Dad. Took me hours to get that look."

"Sorry! Thought you'd just got out of bed." He laughs at his own funniness.

I end up smiling. It's what we do.

My phone pings.

No! Please don't let it be...

It's Katie – phew!

Have fun today, text me later, tell me all about it

Me

Ok. Have fun too x

Katie and Sam are off shopping.

Dad swings in to say bye.

"Bye, Dad. Have fun at the rugby."

"Oh, we will. You have fun too, and remember, Mum will be smiling down today." He gives me a bear hug.

"Don't touch the hair," I warn him.

Dad backs away, holding his hands up. "See you tonight."

And he's gone.

It's 10:11am.

My tummy is doing somersaults again.

How would I actually feel if I knew Jamie was gay?

I set up stuff on the kitchen table. As we're alone it's best to work here, more space and close to drinks and nibbles.

A sketch of a garden falls out of one of the books as I reach to place it on the table. It's of Holbrooke Hall, where Mum based her dissertation; I went with her many times and played while she sketched and studied.

I smile and tell myself I'm not going to cry.

And. I. Don't.

I am so proud.

10:14am.

I look through some more sketches and a picture falls to the floor, of Mum and me sat on the grass. I must have been nine, I guess. I wonder who took it. Or is it a selfie? It could be. We both look happy; Mum is laughing.

I smile.

Still. Not. Crying.

Not sure how I'm not because this is unexpected. I push the picture back into the book of sketches.

10:17am.

I check round the kitchen; I've checked round so many times. Everything is as it should be. Washing up done and stuff put away. I've even run the vacuum round and straightened a cushion.

The kitchen has never looked so tidy, and all for another boy coming to do some studying, who wouldn't even notice if my wet underwear was strewn about drying.

Well, probably not.

10:19.

Should I put some snacks out? Should I just ask what he fancies?

Apart from me!

Ha!

Not going to happen.

It's 10:23am.

I'm making this sound like it's a countdown to something awesome. It could be a countdown to disaster.

I've never felt so nervous about someone coming round, and basically I have no need to, because we're just a couple of mates hanging out doing a history project.

Stop, already!

The doorbell sounds.

He's early. Unless it's not him. Don't be Jordan!

I open the door to Jamie, rucksack over his shoulder, big

smile on his face, white tee-shirt with a picture of a teenager on the front and the logo: 'Some kids are nice. Get over it!'

"I love your tee-shirt." I laugh.

"Using your favourite word, too." Jamie laughs back.

"Yeah, not nice to use the word nice."

That was a good icebreaker. The tension, for me anyway, has lifted. Don't think Jamie is tense about today, by the way, he's acting so coolly.

It's as if I've not met him before. I feel so gawky, so tongue-tied, so silly.

I usher him in to the kitchen. "Can I get you a drink?"

"I'm good thanks, maybe in a bit." He throws his bag down and casts his eye over some of the stuff I have on the table.

"So, this is your mum's stuff then?"

"Yep."

"OK about it?"

"Surprisingly so. Even found a photo I didn't know was there and I've been cool. I'll try and hold it together."

Jamie shrugged. "Don't worry if you don't."

He opens his folder and pulls out some papers. He also opens his laptop and we make a start.

For some reason he has sat on the opposite sofa to where I have my laptop set up. Is that deliberate? Is he making a point?

Stop analysing absolutely everything, Danny! I reprimand myself.

Means I get to look at him from my sofa. I've not seen him without his shirt on.

What?

Why would I have?

What I mean is his tee-shirt fits very well and I imagine him to have quite a fit body beneath his shirt.

I then realise Jamie is staring at me.

"Sorry?" I ask.

"Just asked how you want to start this but you were on another planet." He laughs

I must be blushing.

The morning flies by in a whirl; we haven't even looked at Mum's stuff yet as we have been busy laying down a basic framework.

Jamie stretches. "Time for that drink," he says, rubbing a hand over his head.

"Good idea," I say, heading off to the fridge.

When I come back, Jamie is leafing through one of Mum's picture folders. He looks up and asks, "Is this, like, OK?"

"Sure. Hopefully we can use some of her ideas." I take a seat next to him and I may have purposefully touched his knee with mine before edging away. We look through Mum's work and then the photo I had found earlier slips out as Jamie picks up the book on Holbrooke Hall.

"Is that you?" he asks. Is that a note of surprise?

"It is. I think I was about nine."

"And your mum?"

"Yes." I swallow.

"She looks so beautiful."

I notice his use of the present tense and it gives me a warm feeling.

I agree with him, she did. Lovely blonde hair tied up in a

ponytail falling over her red shirt, and me goofy behind her, looking over her shoulder.

"What a lovely memory to have," Jamie continues. He runs his finger over the picture.

"Thankfully in this day and age we have loads," I say.

"I was going to say you're lucky but that seems totally the wrong word to use. Fortunate is better. You are fortunate to have all these memories."

"I certainly feel lucky to have had the time I did have with her. Of course, I would have liked a lot more time but I guess..." I trail off.

"Is this where she worked?" Jamie finds a picture I hadn't seen earlier. It is of Mum reaching up to prune a rose on the high wall of the garden at Holbrooke Hall. "This place looks amazing too."

"Yes, she based her project on Holbrooke Hall so volunteered there too."

"Do you ever go back to visit?" Jamie asked then instantly put his hands up. "Oh, God, how insensitive of me."

"Not at all. Like the pictures, I have lovely memories of us being there and while some people wouldn't want to be reminded of such things, Dad and I love visiting and feeling the memories come alive." I smile. "We were there just before starting sixth, actually, and we looked at that rose." I pointed to the picture, where Mum was pruning. "It was her favourite."

"I can see why. Almost smell the fragrance from here."

"So much to learn, Jamie," I scolded, then laughed.

"What do you mean?" He looked puzzled.

"Red roses don't have a fragrance. I guess whoever invented the red rose thought they were beautiful enough to not need a scent too."

"I look forward to some tuition."

I laugh. "Careful what you wish for."

We carry on looking at sketches of the Hall.

"Do you think it would be OK to scan some of these sketches in and use them?" Jamie asks. "They really capture what we are after."

"Mum would be so proud. Actually, so would I."

"Should we pick some out?" he asks.

"Yeah, good idea." We spread them about and pick one of the rolling hills looking down to the meandering river. Capability Brown was famous for his views that didn't reveal everything at once, and a clump of trees obscure the view of the full river. You have to go in search of it, which is what we want to portray. Then Jamie picks one up of a row of lime trees bounding the drive. Finally, one of the walled gardens, which shows the way fruit and vegetables were grown in the day.

"It's been really great looking through all these again," I say to him. I hadn't looked at Mum's college work since she had died. I'm rather amazed at how well I'm holding it all together.

"I can tell by the look on your face when you see something." Jamie smiled. "I'm pleased your dad suggested using them."

I look at the clock. It it's 14:46.

"Blimey, look at the time. No wonder my stomach is rumbling."

"Time for a proper break maybe."

"Cheese sandwich? Ham?"

"Happy with anything, Danny. Whatever you come at first in the fridge."

"I'm not doing it all. You can butter the bread."

"Yes, boss." He salutes me.

We take our sandwich, bag of crisps, and a plate with lemon muffins and brownie bites.

We're quiet while we eat. I hadn't realised I was actually starving.

"So," I start, putting my plate on the table next to the sofa, "you transferred up from Basingstoke?"

Did I sense Jamie tensing slightly?

"Yes," he says and there's a pause before he continues. "It's not a secret, you'll find out one day."

I'm sort of intrigued but worried I've asked something he really doesn't want to talk about. "Sorry, Jamie, if you don't want to talk about it it's fine. You've given me plenty of advice. We seem to be digging into each other's pasts and maybe we don't need to."

"No, like you I have to face my demons. It's nowhere near as sad as your story."

Sad?

"Not even sad, really, my story. Mum and Dad were drifting apart and then Mum found out Dad had been on a so-called business trip for a week and taken his secretary with him."

"Yikes."

"Indeed. Silly cow posted some pictures on her Instagram account of them on a beach together. He said the meeting was in Paris."

"Long stroll to a beach in Paris."

"Exactly. They were in Monte Carlo. So, when he got back there was a picture Mum had printed off of them pinned to the front door."

"Nice one," I say.

"He went ballistic. I could not believe he was trying to justify himself. There was nothing he could say to make it right, basically. This was ten months ago. He's moved in with Shirley; he has made no contact with me since then."

"What? It's not your fault, any of this." I am furious.

"I sided with Mum. He thought I should have gone and lived with him and Shirley."

"Was that ever an option for you?"

"No way. He was always drifting about, even before this. I think, really, he should have been a surfer in Cornwall. No ties, no kids."

"A Cornish Jordan," I say, and we both laugh.

"So, Mum said we were moving. She would see him about in the town and get mad, because he thought it was all perfectly normal. At first, we were just moving out of Basingstoke but then Mum said we should have a new start."

"Quite a change, moving up north."

"Yeah, wasn't too sure about it but Mum did say as I would be starting sixth it was like a new start anyway. You know, new kids, big changes and all that, so we looked around and Mallington had a good reputation. Also, Mum could transfer up here with her job."

"Did you say what your mum did?"

"Probably not. Something in education. Advisory role, I think, but she doesn't say much about it. I don't know whether it might compromise her if she did. Bit like a civil servant, I guess."

"OK." I look at him. "So, no other family?"

"Just me and Mum. Bit like just you and your dad. Sorry, I'm assuming that. Maybe you have an older brother or sister at uni or something."

"No, as you say, just me and Dad. Not sure why I don't have any brothers or sisters. It was never talked about."

"So, we moved up in August, got settled and here we are." He throws his arms wide. "In glorious Mallington."

"Hm, not sure glorious is the right word."

"I hadn't even heard of it until July when we were looking for places."

"But you and Mum are happier here?"

"Seem to be. Mum can be a bit, er, well, angry at times. I'm learning to keep my head down when she's off on one. She was always the feisty one and Dad knew when to keep his head down. Doesn't excuse him for what he did though."

"That was like the other day? When you said you'd had a big row?" I ask.

He looks a bit taken aback. "Oh, yes," he says, remembering. "Something had happened at work and she was totally pissed off but then came home the next day and said it was all sorted and had made her look at people in a different light."

"All good now then?"

"Seems to be."

"That's good then." I nod and there is a pause in the conversation.

"OK then," Jamie says, leaning forward on his sofa.

"OK then what?" I ask.

"You and Katie."

"Me and Katie?" I ask worriedly.

"You seem so happy together."

I splutter slightly. "Pepsi gone down the wrong way."

"How long have you been together?"

"We aren't actually, well, you know, together."

Awkward.

"No?" Jamie looks confused. "You both seem so, well, together. I just assumed you were in a relationship. You seem good together."

How WRONG can you be?

I'm not sure how to respond.

What do I tell him?

"We have known each other since primary. Like brother and sister – the sister I never had, I suppose. We do tell each other everything."

"I'm normally quite good at working out this stuff," says Jamie. "Sorry if I offended you."

"No offence taken. Katie will be laughing her socks off when I tell her. She's always trying to get me together with someone." I stop talking abruptly, realising what I have said.

"And has she succeeded?" There is a little evil grin on his face.

"She's trying." My smile has slipped away, along with my confidence.

"Hey," Jamie starts. "Ignore me, I'm sorry if I'm out of order."

There is a pause and I look up at him. "Maybe there's something you need to know."

Why?

Why are you going to tell him?

It's too soon!

You're going to ruin everything.

ABSOLUTELY EVERYTHING!

"Not if you don't want to tell me. Your business is your business."

Stop!

You don't need to tell him.

He has given you a free pass to stop talking.

"You might, well, you know, we have to work together and maybe you won't want to."

Why am I telling him this?

I could have bluffed my way round it.

Today will be the last day we'll spend time together.

"Why wouldn't I want to carry on working with you?" He looks at me in a bemused way. "Oh, shit, you're not a cannibal, are you? Going to eat me like in that comedy programme. Invite me round to watch a video then..." Jamie trails off, leaving the sentence unfinished.

Do NOT say anything.

He has given you a Get-Out-Of-Jail-Free card.

Use it.

Stop talking!

"No, I'm not a cannibal."

Wonderful!

That should do it.

Change the subject.

Stop talking.

Spill your drink.

Anything, just do not tell him.

Pause!

Is that a pause for effect or a pause because I'm about to reveal all to Jamie?

"I'm gay."

What?

I can't believe I've told him.

And there it is.

Out there, just like me now!

No taking it back now.

I could laugh and say, 'Gotcha! Ha-ha. Big fat hairy joke.'

"Right," Jamie says.

I look down at my feet. "So, if you don't want to carry on doing the project, I'll talk to Miss Halshaw and see if we can swap and if you don't want to be here, I'll understand. I should have told you sooner. It was wrong of me. You don't need to stay. I should have said. I don't want to spoil your weekend."

I feel tears pricking my eyes and I keep looking down.

Jamie gets up.

Totally blown that then.

Fuck. Fuck. Fuck.

I should have kept quiet.

How could I have blown this?

Mates would have been preferable to sitting here on my own.

But then…

Jamie hasn't left.

He has come across and sat next to me.

He's sitting on my sofa.

Next to me.

His knee is now touching mine.

He takes my hand.

What is he doing?

Fireworks, mini sparklers going off in my hand, shoot up my arm. I'm having another Marc Laconza moment. This brings it all back; the kiss, the feeling in my tummy.

I look up.

"So," he says, "gay, huh?"

Is he going to punch me?

Call me a faggot?

Rant at me for not telling him on that day in the common room?

Well, apparently not.

He lets go of my hand.

His voice is soft. "Do you want me to leave?"

I look up and he sees my tears. "Have I ruined everything?" I ask.

"Only if you want me to leave," Jamie says. He seems to be struggling to find the words he needs. Is he trying very calmly to tell me to fuck off?

"What do you mean?" I look a little confused.

"I don't want to leave, Danny."

"You don't?"

Now it's Jamie who looks awkward. He has a strange look in his eyes, a look that tells me he is not quite sure what he is going to say next.

"I like you, Danny Ross." He takes my left hand in his. He looks me in the eye and gives a little scared smile.

What. The. Absolute. Fuck. Is. Happening?

He continues. "I didn't think for one moment that was what you were going to tell me."

"No?" I'm slowly realising what is happening.

"That first day I saw you, I thought, 'Wouldn't it be nice if he were...' Well, you know... Oh, wow, Danny."

"You mean?" I am starting to see the light. Might be able to work out an equation but not the simple things in life.

"Yes, you idiot. I was convinced you and Katie were together so I put it right out of my mind."

"Oh God, I thought you must have thought me a right dick. Dropped my book, walked into the chair, lost for words..."

Jamie laughed and squeezed my hand. He held it up. "Sorry. I just sort of grabbed your hand."

"Feels kind of nice," I mumble. "Really nice, actually. Shit. I used the 'N' word twice in one sentence. See what you made me do?" This feels way more than nice, unless you think of the word in ten-foot-high capital letters with gold paint and flashing lights and sparkly bits. Well, you get the idea.

Jamie laughs again.

If he carries on, I am going to turn into a pool of idiotic jelly and slide right off the sofa.

"Bloody hell," Jamie says. "I had no idea we would be talking about this when I came round."

"Me neither, although I was feeling on a high just having you to myself, even if it was doing homework."

"I sort of felt the same. I was so looking forward to today, having had it cancelled so many times. Dreams are..." He started.

"Dreams are CHEAP!" I finish, smiling.

He reaches up and rubs away a stray tear.

"I even tried to touch your hand a couple of times…"

"In maths? OMG, I thought it was an accident. I pulled my hand away. I didn't want to… well, you know."

"I even dropped my pencil on your hand."

"You did!" I exclaim. "That was on purpose?"

"I was testing the water. Have to admit it felt a bit tepid. Sort of confirmed that you and Katie were 'a thing.'"

I laugh.

Jamie laughs.

"Crap!" he says.

"I'm sorry I pulled my hand away. I just didn't think you were gay. I'd convinced myself you weren't."

"I'm just coming to terms with it myself," Jamie started. "You're the only one who knows. I wasn't sure. But now, well, now I am."

"I don't really believe this is happening. Is this really happening? Are you going to jump up and say it's all a lie and the police are outside to cart me off?"

"I'm going with you if they are. We'll ask for a double cell."

All of a sudden, I am terrified.

This is too real now.

Jeez, I've wanted this to happen since I saw him.

Now it has, I feel as though the breath has been pulled from my body.

Like someone just punched me.

"Are you OK?" Jamie asks.

"Just feel a bit breathless all of a sudden."

"Yeah, I think I know what you mean. I was so not expecting this to happen today. Did I say that already? Sorry."

"Is it really happening? What is actually happening?"

Jamie is smiling though. It must all be good.

"I think I just came out to you," I say.

"You certainly did. I think I just did the same." Jamie can't wipe the stupid grin off his face. "Did I just come out to you? Do you feel OK about it?"

"I don't think I've processed it yet. I really was not going to tell you. The little man inside my head was screaming NO at me. Do not tell him, it's too soon, he'll run away."

"My fault because I asked about Katie."

"I'm pleased you did now." I grin stupidly.

Are stupid grins in fashion? Because I feel I would win the stupid grinning contest!

"Definitely." Jamie still had hold of my hand. "I just want to hold your hand. Is this, is this like, OK?"

"It feels amazing," I say. "You have lovely warm hands."

"I can't believe what a couple of idiots we are."

"I'm pleased we did the work first. I don't think I would be able to concentrate at all now."

Jamie nods. "Yeah, totally un-concentratable now, if that is even a word."

"If it's not, it should be."

"So, when you said Katie was trying to set you up with someone?" Jamie leaves the question open ended.

"Yes, she was desperate for you to be gay."

"Her wish is my command." Jamie bows low.

"You will hear her scream from her house when I tell her."

"Are we, are we, well you know, is this a thing?" Jamie asks.

"What do you mean? Do you mean are we a thing?"

"Yes. We announced to each other we are gay, but does that mean, well you know, do you want to be?"

Open ended again.

"Boyfriends?" I ask.

That sounded nice. No. Not nice. Awful word.

It felt awesome!

"Is it too soon for all that?" I continue.

"I'm happy just to be us," Jamie says. "Out and proud. Although, shit, I'm not, only to you I mean."

"Only Katie and Jordan know about me," I announce.

Jamie looks shocked. "You haven't told your dad?"

"No, not yet."

Jamie rubs his thumb over my hand. I don't know if he meant to, but it was like small electric shocks coursing through my body. I felt that if I wasn't sitting down, I would have fallen down, or at least my legs would have given way under me. It doesn't feel anything like I thought it would. My brain is fizzing, my heart pounding, my stomach churning... in a brilliantly excellent way, I hasten to add. And, and, it feels miles better than Marc Laconza holding my hand. Simply because I know this gorgeous boy feels the same way about me as I do about him.

I'm very definitely on cloud nine and a half!

It seems Jamie's having a similar experience. This is just so bloody surreal.

How could I have prepared for this?

All the while, laid on my bed dreaming about Jamie, I had not warned myself I would feel like this. I don't think I could have warned myself. This feeling wasn't on the agenda. I warn you all out there, before you actually embark on your gay journey, you can never know what it's going to feel like because the actual touch of another boy's hand is nothing like you imagine.

"Can I get a hug?" Jamie asks. "A proper gay hug." He laughs.

I know exactly what he means. I want the same. Not just a matey hug.

We hug, a proper big gay hug, holding each other really tight, really close. It didn't need to be anything other than this today. I feel his warm hand on my back through my thin tee-shirt. I rub my hand up and down his back slowly. He pulls my head into his shoulder and caresses my hair.

If my dad hadn't done a good enough job mussing it up then Jamie is certainly trying his hardest, but I couldn't care less. I've no cares in the world right now.

'Mess my hair as much as you want,' I want to tell him. My scalp is tingling at his touch. I could sit here all day; my only care is to be with this amazing boy.

How much are dreams again?

This dreamer has just won the jackpot!

I have a million questions for Jamie. Does he feel the same? I pull out of our hug and look him in the eye. His eyes are so dark, like pools you want to dive into.

"What?" He looks puzzled.

"I want to look at you properly, without thinking I'm having to steal a glance to do it in case I get caught."

Jamie pulls a face. "Look as much as you like, you gay boy!"

I can feel his eyes taking in my face too. My eyes are blue.

"Your eyes sparkle," he says. "Did you know that?"

"Yes, Mum used to call me her little sparkle." I smile at the memory.

Jamie traces his finger down the side of my face and round my cheek. More sparks fly. "I want to ask you so much."

"Me too," I enthuse.

"How long have you known you are gay?" he asks.

"For sure, it was the end of last term." I re-tell the Marc Laconza story. No good hiding stuff from him. "But, once I knew then, I realised I had known for a bit longer, although I hadn't realised, if that makes sense."

"Totally," Jamie said.

"What about you?" I ask.

"Serious answer is a week gone Monday. When I first saw you."

"No shit!" I exclaim. "Do I have that power?"

"You have so much more than that, Danny. When we started chatting, I couldn't concentrate on what anyone was saying."

"Oh, wow, I thought it was just me talking gibberish. Going on about being sad with coffee. FFS."

Jamie laughs. "I know. I thought, 'What is he on?'"

"Really?"

"Yeah, but in such a cool way." Jamie pauses. "But, I guess like you, now I've been thinking about stuff for a couple of weeks, I'm looking back and thinking, 'Yeah, right, that makes sense now.'"

I shake my head, not really believing this is happening.

"So, Katie knows and Jordan knows. About you being gay, I mean."

"Yep, but that's all. I'm sort of out but only to them."

Jamie gives a huge grin. "You are the only one who knows about me."

"I feel special being the one," I say.

"You are so special, Danny. I can't believe I'm sitting here with you, holding your hand, telling you all this. Like, what happens next?"

All of a sudden he looks a bit worried; a frown appears, the smile fades.

I squeeze his hand. "I know exactly what you mean. My first reaction after you told me was, 'Shit, I'm a tiny bit scared now.'"

"Thank goodness it isn't just me."

"Would it have been easier had I been a girl?" I ask him.

He pulls back. "I wouldn't be sat here holding your hand if you were a girl."

We both pull a face.

Then we both laugh.

Who is this boy? Will he be my boy?

I can't stop smiling.

I catch Mum looking at us from above the opposite sofa, a picture of the three of us taken at Centre Parcs when I was eleven. Everyone smiling. We had just been on a bike ride; I had mud smeared on my face where I had come down the hill too fast and taken a tumble. Dad in a space invaders tee-shirt. Mum had chosen the picture and it said so much about us as a family.

"Penny for them?" Jamie breaks me out of my reverie.

I nod at the picture. "Just thinking about Mum. She knows now because she's there looking down on us."

Jamie looks up at the picture. "Mrs Ross, I hope you can be

happy for me and Danny. I promise I'll look after him."

A tear runs down my face. "Stop it," I say but can't help beaming.

CHAPTER 11

Saturday 30th September

Evening

OK, time for you all to calm down.

No, it isn't a dream. Jamie is still gay, I am still gay, I am still happy. Blimey, I'm more than happy.

I hope my bubble isn't going to burst!

What if it does?

I pinch myself to check it isn't a dream.

Shit, that hurt!

Jamie had to go; his mum texted to say she was on her way home and was calling at the pizza shop so he had, like, eighteen minutes to get home. How did she know it was eighteen minutes? Or was that how long his mum took to get pizza and get home? Anyways he's gone, for now.

I am hugging myself and smiling inanely.

I move to clear up Mum's files and place them back in her box. I then put our plates and glasses in the sink and run the water, looking out over the back garden as I wait for it to heat up.

Still smiling. No, not just smiling, I am buzzing, I am fired up. I need 120 beats per minute so I shout across to Alexa, "Play Danny's 120 playlist." This is my upbeat deep house playlist. My friends tell me I have weird taste but this just gets into my head, swirls around and is awesome. Track one starts and I could not have predicted this. It is 'Remembering Your Touch' by Pete Bellis and Tommy. Oh, my, actual… How did it know?

I get Alexa to turn the volume up. The beat is like warm treacle seeping into my brain. I sashay about while I'm washing the pots.

"Someone's in a good mood."

I didn't hear Dad come in.

Well, obviously!

I instruct Alexa to reduce the volume. "How long have you been there?" I ask, slightly breathless.

"Long enough," Dad says, leaning against the door post. "Nice moves, by the way. Seems like someone is in a good mood."

I imagine I have coloured a little. "Good game?" I ask.

"We thrashed them 48-7, and if I'd not been the nominated driver, I may have been slightly worse for wear."

"Plenty of time for that. Do you want me to put the casserole in to heat up?"

"Excellent idea, then you can tell me all about your day." Dad disappears off upstairs.

Can I?

Can I tell Dad about my day?

ALL about my day?

Is he going to figure out there's something up because I

can't stop smiling?

I smile.

Stop it!

No, don't. Keep smiling.

Dad reappears in black joggers and a tee-shirt. Casual wear for Saturday evening.

"How long until it's ready?"

"'Bout twenty minutes."

"OK, shall I put the telly on?"

I pause.

Do I want to tell him?

Maybe I pause too long.

"Something up?" he asks, remote in hand, pointing but not pressing.

I'm still thinking about this but I should have just said everything's fine.

I think he's picked up on it. "Danny?" he asks, now dropping the remote.

"No, I wanted to tell you something. We can talk about it later. It's not important."

Like Hell it isn't, a voice in my head tells me.

Dad comes over and sits at the counter as I'm faffing about putting potatoes on to boil. "We can talk now. Is everything OK?"

Do I just blurt it out?

Seemed to work with Jamie.

"Yeah, all good," I say.

"Do I need a drink?" Dad smiles in his 'everything will be

OK' way.

And I know it will.

"Dad, I'm gay."

There. It is done. It is said. For the second time in one day, it is out there.

There is no pause from Dad, no 'what the fuck', no 'look on his face'. He nearly knocks his stool over as he comes round and gives me the biggest hug.

Two big hugs in one day.

He pulls back and holding my face between his hands he looks into my eyes with that big dad smile and simply says, "I love you, Danny."

I sort of gulp.

"Your mum knew." He looks a little sad for a moment and then it's gone.

"She did?" I ask. "She never said anything."

"I suppose it's not the thing you ask your fourteen-year-old son. I guess she knew you would tell her when you were ready."

I'm sad for an instant, wishing I had been able to tell her this news while I could have, knowing she would have been just like Dad is now, totally accepting of me for who I am. "So, does that mean you've known all this time too?" I ask.

"I never thought about it until your mum said one day, but I haven't been thinking about it ever since. Not looking for reasons to think she was right. Or wrong, even. I'm getting this all wrong now," he says.

"No, you're not," I tell him. "But you're not surprised?"

"Surprised isn't the right word. I'm extremely happy for you."

"You don't mind?"

He gives me another look. "You have to ask? Why on earth would I mind? I want you to be happy. You certainly looked happy when I came in. Oh!"

"Oh?" I ask.

"Has Jamie got anything to do with you being happy?"

Yikes. Can't hide anything from Dad!

"Er, sort of," I blunder. "We weren't doing anything."

"I hope you were." Dad frowns.

What the…?

"You were supposed to be working."

"Oh, I meant, well, yes, we were, we did a load of stuff. A very big load of stuff."

What the fuck am I saying?

A very big load?

Dad laughs. "I know you will have. Sorry, I shouldn't tease."

"Oh, right." My shoulders soften.

"Shit," he says.

"What?"

"The potatoes are about to boil over." He runs round and turns the gas down.

He's smiling that smile again as he turns back. "So, my son, my Danny, falling in love?"

"I don't know about that. We sort of just told each other this afternoon that we, er, we, well I told him I was gay. I thought he would just leave, maybe slap me on the way out."

Dad looks puzzled. "Is that what you boys are into nowadays?"

"No, I mean I didn't know he was gay and he didn't know I was."

"Too complicated." Dad shakes his head.

"Well, it is," I admit. "If you're a boy and go up to a girl and say, 'I fancy you,' she will either swoon…"

"Swoon?" Dad laughs again. "That's probably what happened when Gramps proposed to Gran in about 1970."

"You know what I mean." I punch him playfully on the arm. "What I meant was, you can't just go up to a boy and tell him that, if you don't know he's gay. It could have gone two ways. I wasn't asking if he was gay because I didn't think he was, and when I told him he just sat next to me and took my hand and told me that was the best thing he had heard in ages."

Dad is quiet so I look across and there's a tear in his eye.

"What a lovely thing to say," he says, almost with a break in his voice.

"Yeah, we're going to see if we can commission a short film on Netflix!"

"I'd watch it," he says.

"You certainly would because your son will be starring in it."

"You are unique, Danny. No actor would come up to your standard. You'd have to play yourself!"

I still can't believe this has gone so well. But wait, this is my dad we are talking about.

"So, you're totally cool?" I ask.

"Stop beating yourself up. I am so happy words cannot describe how I feel. I did wonder if you and Katie would ever hook up, but that might have been too intense."

"You think?"

"Yeah, but I'm thinking more about myself. Not sure if I could have stood the pressure."

"Ha blooming ha, Dad," I say but I laugh with him.

"Is she organising the wedding then?"

"She doesn't know."

"Wow, I am honoured. You told me before her."

I don't like to tell him that he just happened to be around when I was in the most infectiously stupidly happy mood, and I had to tell someone.

But I'm kinda pleased I told Dad first.

"Do I get to meet your boyfriend then?" Dad asks, draining the potatoes.

"Of course. I've told him loads about you."

"Like I'm old, forgetful and…"

"None of those things. Dad, you're the best and you know it."

"Aaaaaw! You mentioned him and his mum had moved up north. No dad about then?"

"No, he ran off with his secretary."

"Fresh start then?"

"Yep. I haven't met his mum yet. She does something."

"I would hope she does."

"I mean I've forgotten what Jamie said she did. Probably some boring office job if I can't remember."

"You need to pay attention."

"Yes, Dad. Stop doing my job, by the way. I'm on kitchen duty tonight."

"I was worried you would put sugar in the potatoes and serve custard with the casserole. Thought I'd better take over."

I throw the tea towel at him and he ducks.

Nothing he could say would upset me.

Did I mention I'm floating on air?

Smiling like a total idiot?

I'm not expecting Jamie to go home and tell his mum, which in a way is a shame because I want him to share with someone and be happy. I hope his mum will be as cool as Dad.

So, OK, maybe I'm remembering something that I should have added to my 'Who I Am' page at the very start. I can't remember everything!

I do suffer a little from paranoia. I overthink things and can be a bit screwed up, and Katie or Dad have to reason with me and make me see sense.

So, the thing causing me to be laid on my bed feeling a weensy bit paranoid, is this: what if, and of course it's a big if, what if Jamie's mum goes off on one when he tells her he is gay? What if she sends him off to some boarding school? Well actually, not that, because you hear of such tales at boarding schools – maybe he would like it!

But she could ground him, stop us from seeing each other. She could talk to the school and have us separated.

She could send him to school with an armed security guard to keep us apart.

I've only just found him.

What am I going to do?

Shit, shit, shit!

The voice of reason pokes its head around the door.

"Hey," pipes Jordan, coming into the room.

At least I think it's Jordan; he looks different.

"What happened to you?" I ask, sitting up.

"What? This?" he asks, patting his now short and styled hair, shaved at the sides and back.

"Yes, that."

"Well, I reckoned after what that girl said at M&S..." he starts.

"You have never ever taken any notice of what any girl has said before."

"Yeah, well..." He looks a bit embarrassed.

"Wait." I swing round on the bed. "There isn't a girl, is there?"

"No way," Jordan complains, but there is something.

"It's the girl at M&S, isn't it?" I remember him saying he thought she looked fit and he liked the way she ribbed him about stuff. All I recall is sticking my hand down his trousers to tuck his shirt in innocently. Truly, my lord!

There is silence from Jordan.

"I knew it," I proclaim, although I haven't – it's just that the bell is ringing now.

"I did it for the wedding," Jordan protests.

"Right, secondary reason. The first being the girl."

Jordan looks up at me. "How did you guess?"

"Hm, let me see. I actually didn't until just now, but that's great. Isn't it?"

"I don't know. I haven't said anything to her yet."

"Just been into M&S forty-seven times in the last week?" I

josh him.

"Well, maybe a few. I haven't plucked up the courage."

"You are a man of mystery."

Jordan sits in my swivel chair and does what it says on the tin, going round in a big circle. "Anyways, the wedding went off OK."

"Why are you changing the subject?" I ask.

"So, you don't want to hear about the wedding?"

"Of course, I do, I want to know how many chicks you picked up with that sexy new haircut."

"Chicks and sexy new haircut are never to be used in the same sentence. Especially when it concerns me."

"So? Wedding?" I prompt him.

"It was great actually, and I did get complimented by Auntie Jen and Grandma about my outfit. I reckon Mum thinks you will be in line for a knighthood in the New Year's Honours."

We both laugh.

My tension from earlier has been lifted. I'm sure it will resurface later.

"So, we need a plan to get you to talk to this girl. You could just say 'thank you' to her."

"What do you mean?" Jordan looks puzzled, an expression he used fairly regularly.

"Thank her for suggesting you got your hair cut. Say people think it looks really good and it's all down to her."

"Why didn't I think of that? Brilliant as ever."

"Why thank you." I bow low as Dad comes in with a couple of cans.

"Wasn't sure who this was at the door," he says and laughs.

"Careful, Dad, he's chasing a girl."

"Oh, thought he was another possible suitor for you."

It takes a minute but Jordan looks at me, then looks at Dad, then back to me.

"Shit," Dad says. "You said Jordan knows."

"He does, but he doesn't know you do."

"Wait," Jordan says, holding his hands up. "Head hurting now. Explain rapidly in short words I can understand."

"I'll leave you to it." Dad reverses out of the room then realises he's taking the cans with him so he puts them on the chest by the door.

"Why does your dad know? No, how does your dad know? Who is a suitor? Me?"

"Shut up," I say. But I'm smiling. Was all the paranoia me being stupid? "I told Dad I'm gay. I came out to Dad."

"Fucking wicked." Jordan is on his feet trying to do that finger clicking thing as he dances round in a circle. Sixteen going on six, but I love him. "Seriously? Oh, my absolute... He's obviously totally cool, which of course I knew he would be."

"He's totally cool. We had a bit of an emotional thing but yeah, Dad has a gay son."

Jordan flips round to me again and looks serious. "Why did he say I could be another possible suitor?"

"It must be the haircut." I know I'm blushing again, and of course Jordan picks up on it.

"Stop trying to avoid the question. He said, and I quote, 'another', which to me means there is someone else who might be a possible suitor."

I look at him trying to formulate how all this is happening. But I'm smiling like a loon... again!

He snaps his fingers. "Jamie? Jamie is a possible suitor?" Then he screws his face up again, thinking really hard about stuff. "But why would your dad think that? You wouldn't have said you were chasing a straight guy at school in the hope you could turn him gay." He holds his head.

"Hurting again?" I ask.

"Truly."

"OK, well this might have happened earlier."

He looks at me, open mouthed.

"I told Jamie I was gay."

"Why?" Jordan looks puzzled. "You said that was never on the cards, you didn't want to frighten him away."

"It didn't. He actually took hold of my hand and told me he really liked me."

"In a... in that sort of a way?"

"Yes, in that sort of way."

"Holy craperoonie."

"Indeed. I'm still processing it. But I was just so happy and Dad came in at the right moment and it just sort of came out."

"At least you did. Come out, that is. Wowser, Danny."

"Yes, but as usual I'm worrying about all sorts of stuff, as I do." I shrug and fall back on the bed again.

"Cripes, Danny, you've got a happy dad and a guy who fancies you. What on earth are you panicking about?"

"Just loads of what-ifs. No-one else knows he is gay. Well, Dad does, and now you do."

"And Katie." Jordan looks me in the eye and I'm quiet.

"Katie knows," he says. It's a statement. I'm still quiet. "Katie doesn't know?"

"No," I say in a small voice. "Katie doesn't know."

"Oh no, I'm dead. We need a plan. I cannot possibly know all this before her. I need to go away for a fortnight to some institution and you tell her and make out I don't know and when I come back, she will have your life all sorted out and I'll act surprised when you tell me. How's that? Is that a plan? The best plan? Should I go now and pack a case?"

"Don't be daft. You're my best guy mate. You can get to know stuff before her."

Jordan is shaking his head. "Name the last time I knew anything before her."

I go to speak, then think, then think harder. He's right, of course; she knows everything first and this is major news. If she knew Dad knew about Jamie, then Jordan, she will, well, I'm not sure. "Maybe this news is so big she'll be fine, she will have loads to process."

"I seriously do not need to be around when you tell her. I'll let slip I know or she will ask me something and she will know."

"It could have been her poking her head round my door instead of you, and then she would have known first. It'll be fine." I place my hands on his shoulders. "It will really be so fine. You with your sexy new haircut. She'll be so taken with the new Jordan that she will be fine."

Katie will be fine.

I need to tell her today, like, in the next hour so she doesn't suspect anything.

I ping her and ask if she's around.

She pings back to say yes but needs to get out of the house;

her mother and younger sister are doing her head in. She suggests meeting at the café at the end of Jackson Terrace.

Hm, I think, *not the best place to tell her my news.* She'd scream the place down.

I tell her to come here; I need some help with my English essay.

What a flimsy excuse, I think once I've texted back.

'On my way,' she says.

"OK, Katie on her way."

"Shit. Get me out of here. Can I go out the back way?" Jordan panics.

"Don't be stupid. It will take her fifteen minutes to get here and you go the other way," I say. "She wouldn't recognise you anyway!"

We go downstairs.

"New trainers too?" I feel his forehead. The battered Vans are gone, replaced by Nike-Dunk trainers. OMG, how didn't I see those first? They are so lush.

"Well, you know," he mutters.

"I think they look brilliant," I say, and I mean it. "You went shopping without me, though? I'm hurt. I thought I was your fashion guru." Jordan looks a different type of guy, and I like what I'm seeing. Not in a gay way, just in a, well, in a best friend sort of way, which is after all what we are. "If Jamie weren't around," I start and my eyebrows rise and fall in a suggestive manner.

Jordan looks at me with a sly look. "If Katie wasn't on her way over, right now this minute, I'd be all over you like a rash, man!"

"Get out, you queer boy." I laugh.

"Oh, man, I'm too late now. Knew I should've got this mop cut years ago. We could have made sweet love." Jordan hares off down the road. *Hasn't changed that much*, I think to myself.

"I can't believe you're asking me about English," Katie says, shrugging off her pink jacket. "I'm in the set below you."

"Well before we get down to that, I have something to tell you," I start and before she can go off at an angle surmising all sorts of stuff, which would probably be true, I get back in fast. "I've come out to Dad."

Katie stops in her tracks. "You're joking?" she says but in a good way.

"Nope, it just felt right so I told him."

"And?"

"He didn't kick me out," I say, whirling my arms around my home.

"Well, I never for one moment thought he would have. I bet he was so brilliant about it."

"He was, he was my brilliant dad," I say lifting my shoulders. "He is my brilliant dad!"

And then we are hugging, tears pouring down our faces in joy.

"What did you say then? How did you say it? Did it just come out? Tell me everything."

We sit on the sofa in the family room and I tell her everything.

Well, maybe not quite everything.

Jamie doesn't get a mention.

Not just yet!

And, then, here it comes...

"So, we just need to work on Jamie now." Katie smiles, holding my hands. "He might just be gay, you never know."

"He is," I say.

"Because we don't know for sure. Sorry, what?" she asks, staring at me.

"Jamie is gay."

Another tick in a box.

"Jamie IS gay?" she repeats.

"Yes, you catch on quick."

"How do you know?"

"He told me." I'm so excited I can hardly keep still. I want to jump for joy. I guess Katie is feeling a bit like that too.

"Just like that? Just out of the blue?" Katie squeals.

"Well, I might have told him I was gay."

"You might have? Or you did?"

"I did. I told Jamie I was gay. I told him if he wanted to leave, he could, but he came and sat by me, he took my hand and said he said he really liked me."

"No way!"

"Yes way!" I shout back.

"My work here is done." Katie is jubilant. "I knew he was. I knew this was all going to work out. I knew all along."

And, here's my friend Katie. Katie who knows everything and has it all figured out.

"What an absolute day you've had. Did you think he was gay then, when you told him?"

"No, I just knew I couldn't go on working with him and not tell him. If he found out or I told him later and he was pissed off and asked why I didn't tell him earlier... So that's why I told him."

"Bet you're glad you did now." Katie squeezes my hands.

"You could say." I smile at her. "But in that split second after I told him and he stood up, I thought he was going to leave. Then he sat next to me. I thought my stomach was coming out of my mouth."

The door opens and Dad comes in with bread and milk.

"They're certainly queuing up at the door today," he says, putting his shopping on the table.

"Why?" I ask foolishly, not quite understanding. "Is there someone else outside?"

"No. First Jordan, now Katie."

Silence.

"Shit, I'm having a really good day," he says.

"Jordan was here?" Katie asks.

I don't quite know how to read her. I think Dad is moving to the sofa so he can crawl behind it.

"Er, yeah. Earlier." I squirm. "He came to show me his new haircut."

It wasn't going to cut any mustard, not any at all.

"He knows all this?" She twirls her hand round, encompassing all our chat into a nice glass bowl and giving it a big stir.

"I, er, he, well, he was just..." I start.

"Katie, it's my fault," Dad starts. "I said something to Jordan, not knowing you didn't know."

Silence.

Katie is processing something.

Probably how she's going to kill us both then track down Jordan.

"Actually…" she starts. "Actually, you know what? I think it's good that Jordan got to hear first."

I inhale slightly noisier than I probably should and Dad grips the back of the chair.

"Really?" I ask.

"Sure. Just make sure this is the one and only time this happens." She looks kind of super annoyed but then she laughs. "I can't be mad at you today because it's such amazing news." She turns to my dad and he jumps. I swear, he jumps. "But if this happens again, Charlie, and I find out it was your fault, I will have things to say to you."

"OK, Katie," he says meekly. Then to me, "I told you it was better to be gay. Katie scares me."

We all laugh.

Oh, how we laugh.

I still haven't addressed my paranoia, though, and Katie is the person to deal with this, I think. Put her back at the top of the pile, show her she's really number one.

"Why are you even thinking this?" Katie asks. "You've just had a brilliant day with Jamie and you now think he's going to go home, think it all over and change his mind." I've just told her my worries, and in usual Katie mode she is firing on all cylinders. "Stop over-analysing stuff. Surely, he is going to be super excited like you. Only sad thing is he has no-one to tell." She looks thoughtful for a moment.

"You know what I'm like."

"But you've waited all your life for today to happen, wishing for it to happen, and it has. Be so stupidly happy you can't think straight!"

I can tell Katie is immensely frustrated at my idiotic suggestion that Jamie is now going to run off to Mexico. Hell, running to Manchester would be further than I could deal with.

I need to get a grip.

"I am happy beyond belief but there's a little man sat on my shoulder telling me this isn't right."

"That's bollocks and you know it. What am I going to have to do to prove to you that everything will be fine?"

"I just don't know how his mum will react."

"Probably exactly the same way your dad did. If there's only him and his mum, why would she throw him out or disown him, or marry him off in an arranged fashion?"

I know she's talking perfect sense.

But why hasn't he texted?

I texted him almost as he left to say I was so happy. I hope he is. Couldn't wait to see him again. But nothing in reply.

I check again. He hasn't even read them.

"What?" Katie asked, seeing me grimace.

"He hasn't read my texts."

"Stop overthinking it. There will be a reason."

"But today was the biggest day of my life. Surely he must be feeling the same, but he hasn't said anything."

"He's maybe just too excited to think straight."

I don't want him to be straight!

"You know what I mean," Katie said, reading my mind.

Dad shouted up the stairs. "Katie, do you want to stay for dinner?"

"Oh, shit," I shout.

"What now?" Katie asks.

"I'm supposed to be doing the tea. It was ready ages ago but so many things have happened."

We bound downstairs.

"I kept it hot in the oven," Dad says, "but I'm starving. I know you had important news but we need to eat."

"Sorry." I rush about.

There's a knock at the door.

"Blimey, Piccadilly Circus or what today? I promise, whoever it is, I won't say a single word apart from, 'Do come in.'" Dad heads off while I'm plating up the casserole. Hopefully it'll still be edible.

"I found another stray soul." Dad ushers in Jamie.

What the actual?

I can't read anything from his face.

Has his mum really thrown him out?

"What are you doing back?" I ask.

"No way to treat your boyfriend." Dad laughs.

Everyone looks at everyone.

This is beginning to feel like a very strange situation comedy episode from the 1990s.

"I think I've left my phone here." Jamie is glancing around.

Then everyone's searching around. More sitcom. I hear canned laughter.

Katie suggests we ring it.

Jamie says it's on silent.

I go over to the sofa and check down the back and round

the edges of the seats.

"I think it's an excuse to come back and see you," Dad says.

What is he on? This is my romance. I'm on my knees feeling under the sofa. Then I see the box with all Mum's stuff in. I lift things out and there, down in one corner, is Jamie's phone.

My relief is obviously visible.

"See, there's your reason." Katie is smug.

Jamie looks at me.

"She just thought, well, you know," I babble.

"No, Mr Smarty-pants, you were having the panic attack, not me."

"What about?" Dad asks.

Jamie had opened his phone and seen the messages from me.

"Oh, right," he starts. "You thought I hadn't replied and…"

"No, not at all. Well, maybe a little, but it was all good." I shrug off my paranoia.

"Blimey. Young love," Dad says. "Although I used to be just the same when I was dating your mum. However, mobile phones were like bricks then, you couldn't lose them."

We all laugh and I look shyly across at Jamie to see he is looking at me too, and the look says it all. There goes that butterfly again, trying to get out of my chest, fluttering around, making me feel giddy.

I heave a sigh of relief. Katie had been right. There is always a reason.

"So, Jamie, do you want to eat with us? The number is growing," Dad asks.

"I've eaten, thanks, Mr Ross."

"Well stay anyway, I may have questions." He winks at Katie, who is lapping every minute of this up.

A look of panic briefly crosses Jamie's face.

I pull out the stool next to me and pat the seat. I can't help but touch his hand as he sits down. A smile returns to his face and I mirror it. *Crikey, this is nice*, I think. Nice!

"Dad, Jamie maybe has to be somewhere," I say.

"It would be rude to dash off," he says. "Everyone looked for my phone. Mum won't notice I'm not there. She's preparing some big thing for work. I'm best off out of the way." Jamie gave a laugh. Was it nerves or did he not want to go home?

"OK. Well, welcome, Jamie. We don't stand on ceremony here." Dad points at the fridge. "Fridge, full of drinks of all kinds, please help yourself. Glasses in cupboard to the left."

I catch a look at Jamie. "It's true, he will be hurt if you say no."

"I can do that." Katie jumps up.

"No, Katie, he needs to learn, he won't survive if he doesn't know where the drinks are."

Jamie goes to the fridge, retrieves a Pepsi and a glass and joins us back at the table.

"Quite a day," Dad says after he finishes his mouthful.

"Yes," I muse. "Wouldn't have thought I'd come out to you, and now you're meeting Jamie."

Dad looks at me, puzzled. "No, 48-7 in the rugby. Who saw that coming?"

"Dad!"

"Every time," Dad says, pointing his fork at me.

"I keep trying to teach him," Katie burst out laughing, "but it's fun watching him take the bait."

Jamie is taking this all in but keeping quiet. Maybe he just isn't used to this type of banter.

"Shame Jordan isn't here," Dad adds. "I would have had all my young folk here."

"OK?" I ask Jamie.

"All this just feels so," Jamie looks for the right word, "natural. Yeah, natural, safe and comfortable."

"We try to be happy, Jamie," Dad says. "That's what life should be, happiness."

"Just all a bit surreal, to be honest. Nobody knew about me until today and now you all do."

"Do you feel OK about it all?" Dad asks. "I only found out about Danny today and I couldn't be happier."

"Not sure my mum will be the same." Jamie looks sad for a moment.

"Well, you don't have to say anything straight away. When the time is right, I guess like Danny today, you will know when to tell her."

"Yeah, you're right." But Jamie has a sad look in his eye.

"Anybody got room for cheesecake?" Dad takes a large vanilla one out of its box.

We all put our hands up. Including Jamie.

"Sorry, I seem to have gate-crashed the party. If that's OK," Jamie says. "It looks well amazing.

"Well amazing, it is," Dad says, "and I like people with healthy appetites. Get another plate, Danny."

How can Dad not like this polite boy with a gorgeous smile?

We all sit round the kitchen table quietly eating cheesecake. Jamie has to eat his with his left hand because I am clinging on to his right hand for dear life and I'm not prepared to let go. My hand feels glued to his; the warmth is there, the tingling is back, shooting up my arm when he moves a finger. He looks at me, I look at him. Oh, wow!

There is laughter, there is happiness, there is joy.

Every mealtime in every house should be this way.

The light is starting to fade outside but the glow of my love for this amazing boy is only just starting to grow.

Stop! Just read the story, do not use your imagination.

I realise I've stopped using chapter headings. Are you, dear reader, getting lost? Can you remember what day it is?

Just for you, here goes...

CHAPTER 12

Sunday 1st October

I'm laid in my bed.

I'm feeling pretty damn OK.

I think I slept with a smile on my face.

Jamie and I have texted like crazy young things in love. Just stupid stuff, really, but it all feels so amazing.

Katie keeps texting to ask if it's all a dream. I ask myself that too.

Jordan texted to say he was so disappointed to miss the cheesecake. Ever the romantic!

I hear the front door close; Dad going running.

I glance across at the clock. 9am. Yep, going running.

I should be doing my homework but a few more minutes going over last night won't hurt.

My phone pings.

Yes, again!

Jamie

You awake? X

Me

Yes, just laid here thinking about you x

Jamie

Ooh, nice.

Me

Very xx

Jamie

Same here. Mum says we are going out.

My heart falls. I imagine us walking through cornfields hand in hand, the sun blazing down on our bronzed bodies, sipping cider from a keg.

Really, I truly did.

Me

Shame. Could have hung out.

Jamie

Does she know something?

Me

What like?

I sit up.

Jamie

Just seems we have to do stuff every time I want to see you.

Me

True, but we'll see each other tomorrow.

And we did spend most of yesterday together.

Jamie

Yep

She's calling now.

Am I up FFS

Me

And are you?

Up !!!!!

Jamie

Steady tiger.

Me

Sorry, you do these things to me.

Jamie

By telephone!

I must be good!

Me

You better go

Miss you already x

Jamie

Oh Jeez!

Miss you too x

I flop back on the bed and plan my day, now I'm on my own.

Homework priority otherwise I'll be in the deepest of doo-doo tomorrow.

Better get up.

Oh, I am!

Steady, tiger!

CHAPTER 13

Monday 2nd October

I watch as Jamie enters the common room. Nothing about him is any different today from last week, apart from one thing.

One very large, humungous, ginormous, gargantuan thing.

We both know the other is gay, and that we fancy each other.

I smile across at him and he smiles back.

He leans his hands on the back of the easy chair I am sat in. "Well, a very good Monday morning to you," he says.

"May I wish you the same heartfelt greeting," I say.

"Oh, stop already," Katie says. "Is this how it's going to be from now on?"

"Shush," I say, wagging a finger. "No-one knows yet and also, what is wrong with a bit of common-room romance?"

"Nothing at all, but if I need a bucket because of all this sentimental slush every time you greet each other, well, just saying."

"Not jealous, are we?" Jamie asks.

"Of course, I am." But Katie smiles.

Jordan bounces in, still looking amazing. Mel, engrossed in a conversation with Sam, stops mid-sentence and glances over to us. "Is this Jordan?" she asks.

"Liking the new look?" he asks, twirling round.

"Hmm, fancy a pizza Saturday?" she quips.

"Oh yes, this boy is going places."

"Thought you were going to M&S?" I say to him.

"Might be fully booked. Have to check my planner."

I think he's loving every minute of this.

"So, how are my two boys this wicked Monday?"

Katie holds a hand up. "Please do not join in with all this tomfoolery."

Jordan looks hurt. "What did I do?"

"I've just had all the hearts and roses stuff from these two."

I look from Katie to Jordan and back again. "Will you two please keep your voices down? This is not for public knowledge yet."

Jordan puts his head on Katie's shoulder. "But boys, we is just so damn excited."

Everyone laughs.

First bell sounds and we all jump up.

Jamie and I walk off to history, more DaJa project stuff to deal with. Our fingers accidentally touch as we pass through the door. The sparks fly again and threaten to ignite our hands.

Taking our seats, Jamie looks serious for a moment. "I didn't tell Mum last night." He almost looks apologetic.

"I didn't think you were going to," I say. "Did you change

your mind?"

"I think if it had felt right, I might have done."

There's a pause.

"You're not mad?" he asks.

"Absolutely not." I squeeze his leg under the desk, then thinking better of it I quickly remove my hand. "Sorry. It's really fine. You have to tell her when you feel it's right and if that's not this week, this month, or even this year then that's fine."

"But if she finds out from someone else…" He trails off. He has a slightly sad, indescribable look on his face. I don't quite get it, but hey, he's probably just a bit traumatised.

"Well, how would she? None of us know her, so unless she sees us snogging outside Costa, and as that isn't going to happen just yet, I think we are safe."

"I'd love that," Jamie says, "kissing you in public."

We both smile and I squeeze his leg some more. Then remember where we are again. "Sorry, again!"

"You don't have to be sorry. I'm loving it." Jamie gives an evil grin.

"You do realise we haven't even kissed yet?" I tell him.

"I know, we must put that right. How did that not happen on Saturday?"

"I guess we were just so bound up in the moment of coming out to each other that we must have forgotten. I shall look forward to correcting our oversight."

I'm not sure if we achieved anything substantial in history but we had a good lead on most people by the sound of it.

"A second date?" I ask as Dad tells me he and Sarah are

meeting up again on Wednesday night.

"Mmm, her idea." Dad looks a tiny bit dubious.

"If you don't want to, just tell her. Better to say no now than…"

"Lead her on?"

"No, I was absolutely not going to use those words."

"But that's how it feels," he says, looking downcast.

"Maybe it just means she's not the right one," I offer, passing him a mug of tea.

"Thanks." He takes the mug and gently places it in front of him. "I was thinking, go on this one and I'll know if I'm really not ready."

"OK, but don't pressure yourself." I take a sip from my tea then realise it's still far too hot. "Maybe you need to ask yourself if you really are ready for a relationship, or as you say, maybe Sarah just isn't ticking the boxes."

"Been watching Sex Education again?" he asks.

"Yeah. Of course. I could do Otis' job. I really could."

"Sometimes you have a very wise head on your shoulders."

"Only sometimes, Dad?"

He laughs. "Maybe you and Jamie should celebrate your getting together, take him out somewhere."

"We could do just that." I become thoughtful then look Dad in the eye. "No way! We are not double dating with you and Sarah."

"I wasn't suggesting that at all. Not for one minute."

"Really?" I ask, giving him a look.

"No, but if you wanted to, it may take the pressure off a bit."

"Just ring her and say you're not interested."

"I've said I'll go. Like I say, I'll try a second date then decide."

I'm a bit worried. Dad is trying very hard to get over Mum; not forget her, just move on and have a nice life. Here I am, fallen head over heels in love, well, in something, and want to be with Jamie every spare minute we have. I wish he had felt a connection, but equally, I don't want him to feel he has to date Sarah if there isn't anything there.

I try my tea again. Better.

My phone pings.

Jamie

Just checking in x

Me

Hey, that's cool x

Jamie

U up to anything

Me

Trying to talk Dad out of a second date

Jamie

Not feeling the love?

Me

No, he's really unsure.

Jamie

U think he should cut his losses?

Me

Sort of, don't want to say that coz it might work out.

Jamie

Yeah, maybe he has to make the decision.

Me

What u doing?

Jamie

Just chilling

Me

Dad did suggest something though.

Jamie

????

Me

He said u and me should go out.

Jamie

Out?

Me

A meal

Jamie

Ooh, a date?

Me

Oh very definitely a date!

Sort of celebration.

U fancy it?

Jamie

I fancy you xx

But sure, sounds great

Me

He's out Wednesday.

We could go out same night, save me cooking for myself.

U available?

Jamie

Hang on.

He is obviously checking his calendar. Probably has football.

Jamie

Must be an omen!

Wednesday is the only night I'm free.

It's a date x

Me

Excellent.

Let's chat about it tomorrow.

Jamie

Ok

Jordan

Hey whassup?

Me

Just chilling

I smile to myself at the fact that I'm using the same reply Jamie has just given me.

Me

What about u?

Jordan

Same

Me to Jamie

Having a small chuckle to myself

Jamie

Do tell

Me to Jamie

Jordan just texted

I got to remembering the time I sent you Katie's text

Jamie

Oh yeah!

I was a bit confused

Me to Jamie

Don't need to worry anymore.

If I send you a text saying I love you, then I mean it.

It's for you xx

Jamie

I'm gonna sign off.

Let u guys chat.

Me to Jamie

U don't have to go.

Jamie

I know, but you guys should chat

Catch u later lovely boy xx

My heart swells. I love it when he says such sweet things to me.

Me to Jamie

Ok

Night my handsome young man xx

Jordan

You still there?

Me

Just signing off from Jamie

I'm all yours

Jordan

Aw, I haven't killed the moment?

You weren't having like, phone sex?

Me

No! We were not having that.

Jordan

That just sounds way cool

Love me some of that.

Me

Talking of which…

How's the M&S girl?

Jamie

That's sort of why I texted.

Me

Ok?

Jamie

You're the go to guy.

OK, Dad, so watching Sex Education isn't that bad an idea! I seem to be a bit of a guru, and not just in maths. Everyone, it seems, wants a piece of me. Feels good!

CHAPTER 14

Tuesday 3rd October

Anyways, following our conversation last night, Jordan and I now find ourselves in the Men's Fashion Department in M&S. School is out – so is this boy, ha-ha – and Jordan has the shakes. Lurking behind a stand of fashionable anoraks. I kid you not – who knew anoraks were back in fashion? We are eyeing up the girl Jordan has developed the hots for.

"So, do you have a plan?" Jordan asks me.

"Why have I got to have a plan? You're the one wanting to go out with her."

"But you're the man. You have all the good ideas, you're the best. Look how you worked your magic on my wedding clobber."

I roll my eyes.

Being young, gay, and single is taking a toll on me. I need to work on my own life, but as I look across at this startled little puppy, with his oh-so-sexy new haircut, wanting to be taken in and loved, my heart melts once again.

"OK, well, we can pretend we want to buy something," I start, "then go to try them on. She will notice your new image and instantly fall for your charms."

"Pah! More like I'll run a mile."

"Nothing ventured, nothing gained."

Jordan's eyes are following M&S Girl as she heads off to help a customer.

"You haven't found out her name then?"

"How would I have done that?"

How would I know? I think silently. *Ask her?*

"We can't keep calling her M&S Girl," I complain. "She must have a name badge on; if we go up to her, we can read it."

"OK, good plan." Jordan seems pleased with my basic information. "Then what?"

I grab two shirts off a rack and then his sleeve. "Come on."

"What?" He looks worried. M&S Girl is back at the entrance to the changing room.

We present ourselves and she looks up.

"Hi," I say brightly, probably showing too much tooth in my goofy smile. "Remember us?"

I make a note of her name emblazoned on her badge.

Briony.

She furrows her brow then has a lightbulb moment. "Oh yes, the gay couple."

"No, no, no, no, noooooo," Jordan squeaks. "He's gay," he points at me, "but I'm not gay."

"You seemed to be prepared to welcome him putting his hand down your trousers, if my memory serves me right." But do I see a glint in Briony's eye?

A couple walking past look across then put speed into their exit.

"No, he's just, well, he was just adjusting stuff."

"That what you call it these days?" She laughs. "You make me laugh."

And we had!

"You after more wedding clothes?" she asks.

"Well, Briony," I start. Jordan glances around to see who I'm talking to. He has not clocked her badge, it would seem. Do I have to do everything? "Jordan here," I indicate my learned friend, "he quite fancies trying on these shirts, just for general wear."

Briony looks the shirts over. "That one's fine," she runs her fingers over a blue and white striped one, "but forget the floral."

How could I have picked up a floral shirt? It was the first one I grabbed. We were trying to get our boy away from floral. It was on the list. His mum's list. Absolutely no floral.

"You're right," I say, "bad choice on my part."

"You chose it?" She looks at me questioningly then at Jordan. "I thought you said he was gay."

"He is," Jordan squeaks again. He really needs to get his voice under control.

"Leave that one with me and go and try the striped one on."

Jordan wanders down the line of cubicles looking a bit downtrodden.

"Oh, and Jordan," Briony starts.

Jordan flips round. "Yeah?"

"I like your hair."

Result!

First hurdle crossed.

Jordan disappears. I keep my distance, not wanting to encourage further comments of a gay nature.

"So, you're gay?" Briony asks.

I'm slightly taken aback. "I am, yeah, but trust me, Jordan isn't."

"I would have agreed last time you were here. He was a bit of a mess, but he's certainly putting some effort in." There's a pause. "For someone."

"You're not wrong," I say. "He has, as we say in the trade, the hots for a girl."

What on earth am I saying?

How is this going to help him snare this M&S beauty?

Briony looks at me as if I've just stepped out of a Barbara Cartland novel.

"Sorry, that came out all wrong." I shake my hands.

Jordan comes out of the cubicle with the shirt on. He twirls round.

"You sure he's not gay?" Briony raises an eyebrow.

This isn't going according to plan. But Jordan is, well, just being Jordan. He exudes happiness.

Help me, someone.

Then Jordan comes out with a classic. "If I buy the shirt, would you like to get a pizza?" He looks at her. "Sometime?"

What a chat-up line!

We both hold our breath.

"I cut my hair because you said I should," he continues.

I try to give him a look that says, 'Stop digging.'

"Really?" asks Briony.

"Really," I confirm.

"Really," Jordan confirms my confirmation.

"What if I'm gay," she asks, "like your friend here?"

"We could still have pizza." Jordan looks from her to me. "I often have pizza and other fast food with Danny here, so it's a cool thing to do."

Briony roars with laughter again. "You make me laugh."

Is that her catchphrase? Twice in one visit?

I grab the floral shirt off the rack. "I'm going to put this back, save you the bother." And I dash off.

Up to you now, Jordan Fancy Haircut.

I'm trying to figure out if Katie is a bit pissed off or deliriously happy.

In the space of a couple of days I have nabbed Jamie and Jordan has nabbed Briony, leaving Katie a bit of a 'billy-no-mates'. Well no, actually that's totally wrong because we are all still mates, it's just she has no-one special in her life, but when I ask her about it, she says she really doesn't want anyone, not now; her studies are too important.

"We will so very definitely still hang out and do stuff," I say as we sit together in her bedroom. For someone who comes across as though she takes no bullshit, her room is very pink and fluffy.

"I know we will." She strokes my arm. "We will always be here for each other. Don't forget I've been trying to get you hitched up with someone since last year, so I am more than happy with the result, even if in the end you managed to do it all by yourself!"

"Still couldn't have done it without you." I smile.

"You're smiling a lot these days," Katie smiles back, "which is good. Very good."

"What about our boy too?" I ask her, referring to Jordan.

"I know! Who would have thought? I figured he would have just hung around the skatepark and picked up some female version of himself, but he is maturing into a very well-balanced young man."

Really? Maybe that was a step too far but he seemed to know what he was after now and he and Briony were going for that pizza tonight.

Tomorrow night Jamie and I would be having our first meal as boyfriends. How bloody cool was that going to be?

CHAPTER 15

Wednesday 4th October

Whoa, someone stop this boy from exploding with happiness, and no, I'm not talking about Jordan but I'm sure we will hear all about his evening with Briony.

In he bounces, all aglow, so the evening must have gone well.

The common room is full of sixth formers, all busy with their lives.

Jordan flops into the chair next to me with just a smile on his face.

I know that feeling, truly I do.

"So?" I ask after he has sat there a while without saying anything.

"Well, I had the barbecue chicken one, but then you would have guessed that."

I punched him on the arm. "I am not enquiring about what pizza topping you had. Spill the beans."

"We didn't have any beans. Even I think beans on a pizza would be wrong." Jordan grimaces, then looks at me with raised eyebrows. "Actually, what am I saying? Full English on a pizza base, where in the world have I been hiding?"

I give him one of my looks.

"It was mega. It was awesome. Can you believe she likes Wicked Albatross?"

"Will I need a hat for the wedding?" I enquire. This is solid stuff. I don't know anyone who has even heard of, let alone likes Wicked Albatross, of the famous album I treated him to following the purchase of a wedding outfit.

"Stop already." He playfully flicks his fingers in front of my face. "I think I can safely say I have hooked up with a lovely girl."

A lovely girl?

What the actual?

They will be knitting their own clothes next.

"Briony is so cool. I can't believe it took me so long to ask her out."

"Another brownie point to me, I believe." I score a point in the air.

"You are the man."

"I do believe I am."

"So, your turn tonight?" he asks.

"Yes, but just keep it down. It's just a meal, nothing else. People don't need to know anything further."

"I thought you would have wanted to tell the world."

"We do, but he hasn't told his mum yet and she can't find out from someone else."

"Suppose not." Jordan rubs the back of his head. "Surely, she can't be that bad? Have you met her?"

"Not yet. Seems she's always busy."

Jamie comes in and walks over, a smile on his face.

"You look happy," I observe.

"Going out tonight," he whispers, "and you could say I'm looking forward to it."

My heart swells for the millionth time and sets off my friendly butterfly, who I feel I might call Bobby. Don't ask me why, that just seems a perfect name for a happy little butterfly.

Katie arrives next and sits on the arm of my chair. "How are all my boys this morning?"

Jordan regales her of the events of the previous evening and also adds in that he and Briony are going out again at the weekend.

"My work is almost complete," Katie says.

I don't voice anything but I think I can hold all the glory for getting Jordan and Briony together. Yes, she helped with Jamie but that all came about by accident too.

The day seems to drag by, maybe because I am waiting for the evening to come round.

Last lesson is English, with Miss Waycross who has certainly mellowed a lot and we are perfectly fine now after our recent debacle, although one or two students still think she should be tied to a chair and whipped with a bunch of thorns. I'm sort of hoping that isn't her thing. I can't imagine her being into that. Actually, I can, if I think really hard. I bet it is just, so what she is into!

We are still wading through *The Little Bluebird*, and we have an in-depth discussion about that blasted narrator who really has divided the class into two camps. Some think his views are very biased, me included, and others think he actually makes the story join up. Are we reading the same book?

Miss Waycross eventually gets round to me. "So how about you, Danny? You seem to be in the camp who think the narrator is a redundant force."

"I do, Miss. I think he has his own agenda and having re-read one part three times it makes me wonder if two different people haven't written this book. It seems so disjointed."

Miss Waycross claps her hands. "Hallelujah!" she intones.

Everyone looks round to see what just happened.

"This is exactly what has happened. Well done, Danny, for spotting this. Did no-one else think this might have been the case?"

No-one said anything.

I continue. "He keeps referring to Sandy as a political refugee, although that's not the case at all: then when the story re-starts Sandy clearly has an agenda that isn't understood by her peers." I pause and think for a moment. "So, two people wrote this book?"

"Indeed, and if like Danny you had re-read some parts, it would have become clear."

I feel a bit proud about this. I had only suggested it, I didn't know for sure. Maybe I am good at this sort of thing.

"So, bearing that in mind, now we know someone else wrote the narrator section, what can we glean from this information? Why would someone allow another to be a co-author?"

"Maybe," I start when I realise no-one is going to offer an opinion, "maybe it's because the author wouldn't get the right perspective about the story and it had to come from an outsider."

I think Miss Waycross is going to clap again but she

manages to hold it back.

"Brilliant, Danny."

The bell rings.

"OK, everyone, now we know what we know, I'd like you to re-read the section we have just been talking about so we can discuss in more detail the interaction with Sandy and Malcolm."

We pack up. I'm still feeling pretty damn good about how things have gone this afternoon.

"Swot," Jen laughs as we head out.

"Lucky guess," I whisper, not wanting to let Miss Waycross think I hadn't been 100% certain.

Sixth form is over for the day. The only thing that matters now is going out with Jamie. Bobby my friendly butterfly seems to agree with me and I am walking on air as I leave class. Also, one huge goofy grin is plastered across my stupid face.

Two bathrooms at home are feeling the full force of getting ready to go out. Dad is in his ensuite showering and shaving; I am in the master bathroom showering, but not shaving. Not quite there yet! I have a spot where I don't want a spot so I dab it with some concealer and it just looks like a small skin-coloured bump now. Better, I suppose. I have some special Lynx, called Fever, which is discontinued. Why do they always stop making the best-smelling ones? I found this on eBay for £11, which was a rip-off, and I kept it for special occasions. Basically, it hasn't been used yet! I spray liberally. Is that too much? I sniff. Probably not; it will fade by the time I meet Jamie.

Now, what to wear? What does one wear on a first date? A first date with a very gorgeous boy. A gorgeous boy who doesn't even have to try. Jamie will look drop dead, whatever he chooses to wear. Should I wear DMs or trainers? He likes my DMs. Has he seen me in my green ones? I palm bump my head. Too many decisions. I look at my hair in the mirror. This is going to take some fixing for a start, I think. Ohhhhhhhhhh!

I wonder if Dad is having the same problems. This is his second date with Sarah and he seems OK. I know we discussed him cancelling but he decided to go ahead.

We both come onto the landing at the same time. Dad looks swish in a smart pair of black jeans and a white shirt, black shoes, and his jacket in his hand. I hope I look OK in blue jeans and a checked short-sleeved shirt.

Dad smiles at me. "Looking good, Danny."

"You too, Dad. Feeling OK?"

"Surprisingly, yes. Maybe I was worrying too much."

I follow him downstairs and after some faffing around in the kitchen we both leave the house.

"Sure you don't want a lift anywhere?" Dad asks.

"No thanks. I'm meeting Jamie off the bus by the precinct and it's a bus lane so I'll be fine."

Dad jumps in the car and pulls out of the drive. I turn the opposite way and walk the two hundred yards to the bus stop.

Why is my heart pounding? Not like this is a blind date. I know Jamie. Bobby flutters away madly. Nothing is going to happen tonight. It is just Chinese food and chat with a boy I know. However, that boy is the boy I think I am falling in love with, the boy who does strange things to me with just a smile, strange things that I have never felt before!

The bus arrives and I take my seat by the window. There are only about half a dozen people on it and I don't recognise anyone. Would that have been a problem, had I seen someone I know? I could have walked, I suppose, only about a mile, then I could have composed myself.

What am I talking about? Get. A. Grip!

The bus pulls up by the precinct and I hop off. As my shirt is green and black checked I have put my green DMs on as I had considered, and I pad down the street, round the corner and there he is. Sat on a low wall by the Chinese, looking, well, just looking bloody gorgeous. I know I use that word about him a lot but that's the best word I can think of – he just is. He's just bloody gorgeous. He hasn't seen me. He is watching two girls on the opposite side of the road acting about.

"Hey," I greet him.

He jumps up and instantly gives me one of his smiles. "Hey, I love your shirt."

"Thanks." I clock his pink and blue polo shirt with jeans and trainers. He looks good enough to eat. I want to take his hand. I want to kiss him.

I don't.

I mean, I don't do it, not that I don't want to do it.

It's the written rule at the moment and I'm totally happy with that. I cannot afford to scare this boy off.

He opens the door for me, ever the gentleman, and we go in. I haven't realised he had booked and the young oriental boy, who doesn't look much older than us, shows us to a secluded table in an alcove.

Has he planned this, I wonder?

"Can I bring you some drinks?" he asks politely with a smile.

We order Pepsi and he disappears.

"This is nice," Jamie says, looking round. "Have you been here before?"

"Not for a while. I think it was Gramps who brought us here the last time. What I can remember is that the food is really nice. At least it was. I'm sure it still will be." Why am I prattling on?

"Do you feel, like a bit, you know, weird?" Jamie asks.

"Yes." I relax. He is obviously feeling the same. "Don't know why. I'm with you and that's all I want."

Jamie reaches under the table and touches my knee. Fireworks up my leg, just a simple touch. Oh, wow! "You say the loveliest things."

Le Wei comes over with our drinks. I'm getting pretty good at reading name badges now.

Ha!

He places them down and asks if we need a little more time before ordering. To be honest we haven't even opened the menus so we apologise and he gives a short bow and says he will return.

"Aren't Chinese names supposed to mean something?" I ask as he retreats.

"I think so." Jamie gets out his phone and is Googling in no time at all. How did we ever cope without the fricking internet?

"Beautiful and extraordinary," he says, turning his phone around.

"He is quite striking," I say.

"Oh, yes? You looking?"

I am caught on the hop momentarily. "Oh, no, I only mean he is living up to his name."

Jamie laughs. "Only messing. It's good to admire other people, and I agree with you."

Le Wei returns when he sees we have stopped checking the menu and we order crispy duck, sizzling chicken with spring onion and ginger, sweet and sour chicken, and egg fried rice.

"I haven't had crispy duck for ages," Jamie says and I swear he is licking his lips. "It's making me feel very hungry."

Le Wei is by the table again. He places a bowl of prawn crackers between us and clears the bowls to one side. He slides off again like a phantom and returns with a lit candle, which he places in the centre of the table.

"Ooh," I say, wide-eyed, after he has gone. "Does everyone get a candle?"

"Only the gay boys that he likes the look of." Jamie smiles.

"Really?"

"Who knows? We'll have to keep an eye out to see if other tables get them."

I really want to reach my hand across the table and just let my finger touch his. I'm struggling not to do it. Our hands are only inches apart. I think Jamie probably wants it too but I don't push it.

"You'll never guess," I start, changing the subject.

"What? Do tell." Jamie leans in.

"I was told I was brilliant in English today."

I register something strange in Jamie's look but he is full of praise. It seems when I mention English classes he seems to look a bit vacant. It has happened before, when I had the row with Miss Waycross.

"What did you do?" he asks, and he does now seem genuinely interested after his lapse of concentration.

"We were discussing this book called *The Little Bluebird* and I was the only one who realised that two people had written it."

"Well done you. I'm proud of you."

"How was your afternoon? Anything riveting?"

"Economics, so no, very boring. Don't know why I'm doing it, really. Just couldn't wait to get out so I could start getting ready for tonight."

We grin like loons at each other. I may just have won the competition again.

Le Wei is here again. How does he do it? This time he places hot plates with candles in them, which will keep our food hot. The duck follows and he expertly shreds it. Jamie says it is very professionally done and Le Wei politely thanks him and says it is the most popular dish on the menu.

He retreats and we start to roll pancakes with hoi sin sauce and the duck.

"Do you like cucumber?" I ask, pushing the bowl of sliced salad towards him.

"I don't mind but to be honest I would never put it in these pancakes, it would totally spoil the taste."

We abandon the bowl, thankfully. I am most definitely in the 'I hate cucumber' camp!

The duck is unbelievable. So tasty, melts in the mouth and plenty of crispy skin too.

"Yum," I say, pushing the remainder of the first one into my mouth.

"This is so good," Jamie says and gives me a look.

Oh, stop!

All he has to do is look in my eyes, those big brown eyes, smiling eyes.

The meal is a total success. Our feet find each other and at one point when no-one is around Jamie does touch my hand with his fingers and looks at me. I beam and don't pull my hand away. I don't want this night to end.

Le Wei clears our dishes and asks if we would like dessert.

"I think we are stuffed," I say, patting my stomach.

"Maybe a sharing dessert?" He smiles at us both. "One plate, two spoons?"

We look at each other.

"What do you think?" I ask Jamie.

"Sounds good," he says.

"This is your first date?" Le Wei enquiries politely.

Like, what just happened?

Even if it wasn't, you couldn't complain as he is just so damn polite and he is beautiful, and it turns out he is also extraordinary. His parents chose well when they named their son.

"Is it obvious?" I whisper.

He leans in between us. "You look so good together. I'm pleased I was right."

"Shit, does that mean that everyone in here knows?" Jamie asks after Le Wei has headed back to the kitchen to get our sharing dessert with two spoons.

"Nope, he's just extraordinary."

"But dead right," I say, nodding.

Jamie lets his foot go up the outside of my leg. Every touch is like an electric shock. I am secretly hoping we might end the night with a kiss. Or two.

While we wait for our dessert, I ask Jamie about the first time we met.

"OK," I start, "when we first saw each other I seem to remember acting like an absolute halfwit."

Jamie looks into my eyes, smiling. "You mean the bit where you dropped your book? Or the bit where you stubbed your toe on your chair? Or the bit where you mixed your words up?"

"Yeah, right," I say. "So, I wasn't at my best."

"Because I had walked in?"

"Indeed. I had never seen such a gorgeous specimen." There's that word again! "I just thought, wow! I was lost for words."

"Well, not lost." Jamie wags a finger at me. "You just couldn't get them out in the right order. I have to say, I loved it. At the time I thought you were just very shy."

"I am," I protest. "I still am," I add quietly.

"Another thing I loved." Jamie traces his finger on the tablecloth, maybe enticing me to touch his fingers.

"Another thing? How many things were there that day?" I ask, still loving every minute of this story.

"Well, I loved your hair, still do. Messy but so groomed. I loved your DMs, still do," he says, laughing. "I will get to try some on one day."

Oh, my goodness, he likes my DMs? Well, I think he might have mentioned that before. "Go on," I prompt.

"I loved your crazy smile, those blue eyes, so deep, and I just thought, 'I wonder?'"

"And you were right," I say, feeling breathless.

"I was right."

"And all those little hints, messages," he says, reminding me of his attempts to find out if I was gay too. "I was starting to think you weren't and I'd just have to hope to be friends."

"Me too. It's just amazing we were on the same wavelength but too scared to ask."

We both go quiet then Le Wei arrives with the dessert. To be honest, it looks like two desserts on one plate. I think he likes us.

The dessert is a success; our two spoons clear the plate and all too soon it is over.

"I've had the absolute best night of my life," Jamie admits to me.

"Me too," I agree. "Wish it didn't have to end." I look a little sad and pout my lower lip in jest.

"Hopefully this is just the start of us." Jamie looks thoughtful.

Us?

Oh wow!

Yes, please, please let there be an US!

We head to the door having paid the bill.

Le Wei is waiting to open it for us. "I hope we see you again very soon." He beams that extraordinary smile at us.

"I'm sure you will," I say. "We've had a lovely evening. Thank you."

Le Wei bows again and heads back into the restaurant, probably to charm the next couple.

I zip up my blue padded jacket and Jamie pulls his denim jacket closer. He even rocks double denim.

"You fancy walking the long way back to the bus stop?" Jamie asks. We have different buses from the same stop.

"Sure, that sounds great."

We cross and head down the tree-lined road, with the

canal slightly below us. We walk slowly, in silence for a while.

"I've had the best night," I say to him again. I need to tell him how good it has been.

"Same here," Jamie starts.

"I feel there's a 'but' coming. You're not still worrying about telling your mum? Because if you are, I've told you we can just be cool. No rush, no panic." I so want to hold his hand right now, but there are people everywhere and the lighting is quite bright in the street. Damn you, streetlights!

"But I owe it to her to tell her." Jamie shrugs, pushing his hands deep into his pockets.

"Do you not think she will be fine?" I ask, remembering my dad's instant reaction. "I know everyone deals with things differently." I don't want to push him.

"I'm sure she will be fine but she does sometimes flare up at stuff. She tells me afterwards that it's a 'woman thing.'"

I screw my face up.

We turn and cross the canal, and turn again to walk down the far side. There are barges moored here; people live in them. I sometimes wonder what it would be like to live in one. I wonder what it would be like to live in one with Jamie – no cares in the world, just pootling about on the water. I smile at the thought.

"Penny for your thoughts." Jamie looks me in the face.

I point at the barge. "Just wondering what it would be like to live on one."

"Bloody cold, I bet," Jamie says, bursting the bubble.

"Yeah, you're probably right."

We pass by a pub on the far bank, which has hardy souls sat outside, mainly smokers by the look of it. Then some industrial units, a small carpark next to a row of shops, then across the canal again to head up the short hill to the main road and our bus stop.

We pass my favourite charity shop, which has the best selection of second-hand books in the town, then as we approach three restaurants in a row, there is Dad. He is stood on the pavement. My heart lurches. Has his date gone wrong when mine has been like a huge piece of apple pie with custard oozing down the side? Please, tell me not.

"Hey, Mr Ross," Jamie says, seeing him the same time I do.

"Hey, boys, have you had a good night?"

"Brilliant," I start. "How about you?"

"We've had a good night. Sarah forgot her scarf and has gone back in to retrieve it." He indicates the Indian restaurant. "Maybe you should meet her? Might seem strange if you're just heading past and not say hello."

"Can do, but she doesn't know us so she wouldn't know if we just walk past."

Then one of the most surreal moments in my life takes place.

Dad is standing with his back to the restaurant and Jamie and I are facing it.

Adjusting her scarf as she comes out of the restaurant, is Miss Waycross. At first, I think she has probably been in for a meal for one on a Wednesday night and is just coming out, and will turn the other way. I then do a double take as she approaches Dad, not having seen me.

She is two paces away when she spots us and her step falters.

"Miss Waycross," I say, not really knowing what else to say. Has Dad just been on a date with my English teacher? No, not possible, I would have known. Dad would have known and Miss Waycross would have known. My palms feel a bit sticky. Should I be concerned?

Surely someone would have known.

Thousands of random thoughts race through my brain. Did she know Dad was my dad? Surname? He must have mentioned having a son called Danny. She taught a Danny Ross! Had wheels not turned, cogs bound together, answers?

Dad looks at Miss Waycross and repeats my words with a question mark at the end. "Miss Waycross?"

Jamie is noticeable by his silence.

Smiles have been removed from all our faces apart from Dad's at the moment. Is he the only one who isn't connecting any dots?

I look at Jamie and wonder why he is so quiet.

A chill wind blows across from the canal.

"You two know each other?" Dad asks.

"Miss Waycross is my English teacher."

Dad visibly blanches. "But, Miss Waycross?" he asks again. "I thought your name was Sarah Walton." Dad is confused, now so am I.

"I use my maiden name for teaching," Miss Walton or Miss Waycross says. Looks like she is doing a grand job of thinking on her feet. I think of *The Little Bluebird*. Written by two people. The story unfolding in front of me is of two people.

Still, what the actual fuck? My dad is going out with my English teacher.

I turn to Jamie to say something about this point to see he is ashen white. "Are you OK?" I ask quietly. "You look awful." I want to grab his hand, then give him a hug, but he's not out to anyone yet so I hold back.

Sarah breaks the silence. "So, Danny, your dad tells me you were celebrating with your boyfriend tonight? First date and all that." She seems to have composed herself nicely, and looks first at me, then at Jamie.

"Er, well, yes." I turn to look at Jamie again and wonder why he is so pale.

"Are you not going to introduce us, Jamie?" she asks, looking at Jamie. "I assume Danny is your boyfriend." Her tone seems a little bitter.

Jamie is going to introduce us? What does she mean? She doesn't teach him. I'm having a moment trying to comprehend just what is going on, and then…

"Stop it!" Jamie shouts.

I step back. What just happened. "Jamie?" I ask.

It's quite dark but I'm sure I see a tear glistening on his cheek.

Dad reaches out to Jamie. "Are you OK, Jamie?"

Miss W. has raised her eyebrows.

In a smaller voice, Jamie continues. "Stop it, Mum."

I did not see the shovel coming down the road, but it smacked me right between the eyes and I stagger.

"Mum?" I choke the word out.

"Mum?" Dad says, a little bewildered.

My head is in a whirl.

So, my dad is not only dating my English teacher, but she also happens to be Jamie's mum. Which is a bigger pile of crap than her being my teacher.

You are having a bloody laugh.

Maybe I misheard.

I turn to face Jamie. "Miss Waycross is your mum?"

He is downcast. "Yes," he says in a small voice. I can hardly hear him.

My chest is heaving up and down. I have so many damn questions but my brain won't form the words. They have all been thrown in the air like little pieces of delicate confetti and they are swirling around, not wanting to couple up to form sentences.

I've just had the best night of my life, the VERY best night of my whole sixteen-year life on this planet, and now I don't know who any of these people are.

Nobody is talking.

Why is nobody saying anything?

Tears are bubbling up in my eyes.

Everything is ruined.

My life even flashes before my eyes. I met this guy, this gorgeous guy. We went on a date, it was perfect, and now all I want to do is jump in the canal.

"What's going on?" I ask no-one in particular. Anyone can chip in with an answer, I don't mind who starts. Just so long as this pain in my chest goes away and this nightmare will end.

Then Dad asks me if I'm alright. The words sort of wash over me before I realise what he's asked.

I want to scream in their faces that no, I am not alright.

My dad is dating my best friend's mum, who also happens to be my English teacher. I told Jamie loads of stuff about her when she verbally attacked me and he never said anything about her being his mum.

I narrow my eyes. I seem to have moved around so that I am actually looking at all three of them. It feels a bit like them versus me. "I don't know what I'm feeling right now," I say to them.

I think Jamie can tell by the look on my face what I'm thinking. "Danny, I'm sorry, I couldn't," he starts.

"Couldn't what? Couldn't tell me that this," I point to Miss W., "is your mum?"

I just look at him. This gorgeous boy, this boy with the smile that melted my heart. He is a liar. He is crying now, but I don't go to him. I don't know what to do.

I'm so confused. All of a sudden, I turn and run.

I need to process this without an audience.

"Danny!" Dad shouts.

I just run. I don't hear footsteps; no-one is chasing after me.

Jamie doesn't come after me. He doesn't call out.

I don't turn round. I don't want to see him still rooted to the spot.

Does he not care?

What's happening?

I keep running until I can run no more and I can't see through my own tears. My chest is burning with the pain of running flat out. I get a few strange looks as I charge down the road, turn down a side path and end up back at the canal.

How has this night ended in total shitty awfulness?

I sit on a bench by the dark water. I close my eyes and try to get my breathing under control. There is no sound at all, the murky water is still, no-one is walking along the towpath.

Jamie and I walked along the towpath only moments ago. How different things seem now. I look at my hands, still shaking, not just with the effort of running but with the shock of what I've just learnt.

On Saturday I came out to Jamie, then to Dad. It had been

my moment and I felt so bloody amazing. It was all for nothing. What had been the point? I don't have a boyfriend anymore. I never want to have a boyfriend.

Then the cold realisation of what I'm saying hits me and I let out a cry of anguish. This is what I have wanted ever since I knew I was gay. Katie is constantly trying to get me hooked up. I had managed to do just that, almost without her help. I thought I was sorted.

I bury my head in my hands and let tears take over. I just hope nobody is about. I don't want a comforting hand on my shoulder. I need to let this out.

Then I hear the church clock striking ten. The last bus home will have gone. I don't want to ask anyone to come for me, I'm not ready for that yet – sympathy, how sorry everyone is, there'll be another boy. I don't want another boy. I realise I still want Jamie, but I don't think that's going to be an option now.

I stand up and pull my hood up to hide from the world and start to plod along the canal.

Then I feel guilt. None of this is Dad's fault. I know he'll only worry so I should go home. I could text him to say I'm on my way. I pull my phone out; it's been on silent because of being in the restaurant and there are three texts from Dad.

Danny, where are you?

Danny, please call me

Danny?

There's a missed call, too. I don't want to talk to him on the phone so I just text to say I'm OK and I'm on my way home.

Why hasn't Jamie texted?

It's the longest mile of my life. I feel like I'm walking

through deep mud, my feet scuffing on the towpath. I cross the last bridge and head up to the main road.

I love Jamie, don't I?

Does he love me?

Why hasn't he texted?

I'm trying to go back through conversations we had, which had included me talking about his mum, and not once did I detect any weirdness. Oh, wait, that time in class when he went quiet. Was that significant? Then the day after I'd argued with his mum and he was off with me, he said I should have told him about the argument. Of course I didn't need to, because in a roundabout way his mum had told Jamie of the argument. Just not that it was with me. But when I told him the next day, he obviously put two and two together.

Shit!

Now I start to feel angry. Angry at Jamie. If we're supposed to be a couple, why did he not tell me about his mum? He could have explained stuff after we came out to each other. He could have simply said, 'I have something I need to tell you. Your English teacher is my mum. I couldn't tell you before but now we're an item you need to know.' I would have still been a bit freaked out about it, but he would have told me. He would have told me. Not his mum, not in the street, not with Dad there, not with me wondering what was going on. Not making a fool out of me.

Is it Jamie's fault?

I stop about two hundred metres away from home and try to shake all the feelings in my head into order.

Seriously, Danny, do you still want to be with Jamie? Simple question. Yes, or no. Why is the answer forming in my head, 'I don't know'?

I set off again and before I know it Dad is by my side.

I fall into his arms, sobbing.

"Come on, let's get you in."

I say nothing, I can't talk. Everything has been knocked out of me. I don't know if I ever want to talk again.

I know I will, though.

Why hasn't Jamie texted?

Dad shuts the door and we go through to the kitchen.

He holds my face between his hands and watches the tears roll down my face. Then he pulls me close and gives me his 'it'll be fine' bearhug. It goes on until I pull away.

"What happened, Dad?" I ask.

"A whole lot by the look of it, but it can be sorted."

"How? How can anything be salvaged from this?" The words catch in my throat. "Jamie didn't even come after me. Does that not show what he thinks?"

"I think he was totally knocked out by it all. He didn't know about me and his mum. Well, no-one knew anything about anyone really."

"He knew she was my English teacher for fuck's sake," I snap. Then regret it instantly. "I'm sorry, Dad. That was uncalled for. But out of us all, Jamie knew that. He knew the link."

"Understandable in the circumstances." He still held my shoulders.

"We had the best night. It's ruined."

Dad shook his head. "It doesn't have to be ruined. If you had the best night, then it can be repaired. If you love him, then..." he starts.

"I don't know that I do love him."

Why hasn't he texted? Anything? Just to say sorry! Does

he have to be sorry? Is he sorry even?

What am I saying? I still feel like I worship the ground he walks on. How can I throw that away? Isn't love stronger than that?

"Did Jamie go off with his mum?"

"I drove them back home."

Wow, ever the gallant hero. I feel like snapping but hold my tongue.

"His mum is the one with all the lies, Danny. Working under three names."

"Three?" I shout.

"Her name is actually Sally Burton."

I'm not quite taking this in. Why would you need three names? "Three names? Is she on witness protection? Running from the police?"

I feel as though I'm in the middle of a most bizarre novel, or a drama series you might see on TV and constantly comment that this wouldn't happen, yet here we are in Dannyworld and it is happening. It is happening to me.

"Did she know I was the Danny Ross in her class? Did you talk about me? She must have made the connection." I'm grasping at anything to make this seem plausible. "How could she not know?"

"I didn't know she was a teacher, Danny. She said she was an author."

"Another lie."

Dad nods his head. "But don't take this out on Jamie."

"He knew about the teacher stuff. Did she tell him she was dating you, I wonder? Did he know that too?"

"He would have told you."

"I'm beginning to wonder."

I snatch my phone out of my pocket.

"He hasn't texted. It's been over an hour."

"Remember the last time he didn't text? There was a perfectly good explanation. Why don't you text him?"

"No way. This is his mess."

"I thought you loved him?" Dad says gently.

"I did," I sob.

"You do," Dad says, massaging my shoulders. "Don't let this spoil it. Maybe leave things until tomorrow. Talk to him at school."

"Why do you know everything, Dad?" I ask. Yes, that was a perfectly rational thing to say but I could only see anger.

"I'm the adult," he says. "Let's think about how Mum would have handled it."

We both hold each other.

I wake with a jolt. It's 03:07am when my eyes focus and glance at the luminous face of my clock. I lay a while, wondering if Jamie is asleep. I pick up my phone and check messages; the green circle has an eight in it. My heart leaps. Has he texted? I click on messages.

Six from Katie, two from Jordan. I slump again. Why isn't he saying something? Anything!

Do I want him to say sorry? Dad said it wasn't his fault, but I feel it is.

Am I being totally thoughtless, ungracious?

I check Katie's messages.

How did tonight go?

Guess you are doing boy on boy stuff!

Had a good time?

That good you can't tell me?

I need feedback!

Danny?

See you tomorrow!?!

Oh, crap. I'll be in bother now. I just hadn't seen them. Oh well, my life can't be any worse, I reckon.

Is all this just too quick, too soon?

Maybe it's a sign.

But!

I have never ever felt so good as I did only a few short hours ago. I want this boy in my life, this gorgeous boy!

I throw my phone down and turn over.

CHAPTER 16

Thursday 5th October

I text Katie and ask if we can meet at the crossing and walk to school together. She replies 'yes' but nothing further. She knows me well enough to understand that I have sensitive information and need to talk to her about it.

Sure enough, Katie is by the crossing when I turn the corner.

"OK?" she asks as I approach. "I don't like crossing meetings, usually means something is up."

"Could be nothing," I mumble.

"Spill," she says, linking arms, and we begin the quarter-mile walk.

"OK, but don't let me cry. I don't want motorists thinking my dog has died."

"You don't have…" Katie starts, but then realises.

"OK, so Dad had a second date last night."

"Yep."

"I met her, by chance, outside the restaurant."

"OK." Katie knows to just let me get to where I need to be

in my own time. Questions will be answered later.

"Dad is dating my English teacher."

Katie grinds to a halt. "Miss Waycross?"

"Yes."

"No!"

"Yes!"

"But you and her had that thing."

"Yes, but we sorted that."

"OK, so how do you feel about this?"

"Well, that's not all."

"Oh! There's something else?" We are still rooted to the spot.

I look her in the eye. "She is also Jamie's mum."

The world stops. Cars and buses silently drift past. I can see Katie trying to process this, trying to find answers to the questions in her head.

"No," she says, so quietly. That is all she can think of. "No."

"Yes."

"But," she starts, "how? I mean, we don't know this, do we?"

"No."

She closes her eyes. "I'm still…" She starts again, then stops. "I can't make sense of this. She is dating your dad, must have known you were his son, knows she is your teacher but has told your dad she is an author." She looks into my eyes. "He didn't twig anything with the name?"

"Her name? She calls herself Sarah Walton to Dad, Sarah Waycross to us at school, but her name is actually Sally Burton."

"Is that even allowed?" Katie looks incredulous. "Three

names, FFS?"

"So, nobody knew," I say, then hold a finger up. "Apart from Jamie."

Katie pulls me to a stop again. "What? Jamie knew your dad was dating his mum?"

"Well, no, not that."

"Jamie knew what then?"

"He knew that his mum was teaching me English and never said a word about it."

Katie looks down as we slowly start to walk again. "There has to be a reason."

"You'd think," I say.

She pulls me to a stop again. "How are you and Jamie then? Oh, shit! You are still, well, still a thing?"

"I don't know. I haven't heard anything from him."

Katie shakes her head. "No, please don't let this be happening. I just got you two together. How was it left? Was Jamie with you when you saw his mum? We really should not go to school today, I have so much to do."

"Stop. I actually ran away."

"You did what exactly?" Katie looks at me as though I just lost my mind.

"We were all stood there, I'd just realised my dad was dating Sarah, or Sally, then Jamie just blurts out that she is his mum."

Katie holds my arm.

"I just ran off. I couldn't deal with it." I look downcast but I'm all cried out. "Jamie didn't even call out. He didn't run after me. He hasn't texted. I haven't heard a thing from him."

Katie lets out a big sigh. "It's Friday," she announces.

"Aha," I say, thinking about Jordan.

"Maths first lesson. You and he have got to talk about this."

"Shit. My mind is all over the place. I'm on autopilot, haven't even thought about maths."

What am I going to do?

I am going to be grown-up about it, that's what I am going to do.

"You do still like him?" is all Katie has to say, and I can feel tears rising.

I close my eyes to blink them away. "I do, yes. I can't just stop feeling the way I do about him."

"Then it will all sort itself out."

We reach the gates. I need to compose myself so I tell her to leave me so I can breathe.

I almost crash into Miss Wilson as we both round the corner of the corridor leading to the maths room.

"Sorry, Danny," she laughs, "both on the verge of lateness."

"Yes, Miss, sorry too." I wave her into the classroom.

I follow.

Jamie is not there.

Later than me.

I take my seat.

The final bell sounds.

"No Jamie today?" asks Miss Wilson as she takes the register.

I shrug.

"What do you mean he wasn't in class?" Katie asks in a whisper as I tell her in the common room.

"What don't you understand about the statement 'Jamie was not in class'?"

I wonder if his mum is here today. I didn't have English today and I haven't seen her, not that I've been looking out for her.

"We need to find out."

"Why?"

"Well, if they are both not here," she starts.

Shit!

Oh, shit!!

Have they packed a bag and returned to Basingstoke? Could his mum not deal with, well, what was it she could not deal with?"

But then bizarrely, and a lot of really bizarre things seem to have happened so far, there is Miss Waycross having just entered the common room, and she is animatedly talking to someone I'm not familiar with. I slide down further in my seat.

"Do we say something to her?" asks Katie.

"We most certainly do not. She maybe thinks he is here somewhere. Don't want him in any deeper bother than he may already be."

"OK." Katie turns away and we look down at the floor, me glancing up occasionally, until she retreats out of the room, almost knocking Jordan over in the process.

He skids to a stop and looks round. "Where is our Loverboy?"

"We don't know," we both chorus.

"All good?" he asks, his smile fading.

"We don't know," in time again.

Jordan screws up his face. "Do I need to know?"

"Probably best you don't just yet," Katie tells him.

"We did have a great meal though," I say, deciding I'm not going to write off last night because I had had an absolute blast. "The waiter even asked if it was our first date."

"Hope it wasn't your only one by the look on your faces." He indicates our glum looks.

Jamie doesn't make an appearance all day and Katie and I once again walk back as far as the crossing.

"You want me to walk home with you?" she asks.

"No, I'll be fine."

I had relented and texted Jamie but he hasn't even looked at the two messages I sent.

I simply said:

I missed you today, are you ok?

I really enjoyed last night x

Where is he?

Has his mother locked him in the cellar?

Does his house have a cellar?

I am imagining chains clanking.

Stop it!

CHAPTER 17

Jamie

OK, readers, I need your help here. I really need to know what's going on, and not being able to wait until things are sorted out, which could be, like, forever, we are going over to Jamie's house to find out. Well, I'm not going, but you are and I really need you to report back.

Dad had dropped Sarah and Jamie off while I was literally on another planet, well, down by the canal questioning my life.

The journey to Jamie's house had been undertaken mostly in silence. Jamie sat in the back, and as Dad kept having a sneaky look in the mirror, he could see Jamie still looked shellshocked. Sarah/Sally had stared out of the side window, not wanting to engage in conversation. Dad remembered when Danny had told him he was gay. He had been overjoyed, yet here was Jamie's mum, like an ice maiden. What was wrong with her?

He pulled into their drive. He had hardly pulled the car to a stop when Sarah/Sally began to take her seatbelt off.

"Sarah," he started.

She cut him off. "Thanks for the lift, Charlie. See you around."

Jamie was still sat in the car. She opened his door and gestured him out.

Dad sat with a stunned look on his face as they headed up the steps to their home. He was wondering about rushing after them but thought they maybe needed some space. He was just a bit worried that Jamie was going to come off worse in this confrontation, and it wasn't fair. He was a good kid. Also, he had other worries. Danny had dashed off and he didn't know where he was.

Jamie had done a bit of thinking in the car in the total silence. His mum had to realise that he had this huge thing for Danny. He still didn't know what that was; all he knew was that in Danny's presence he felt amazing. Danny had some sort of power over him and he wasn't willing to give him up without a fight.

Sarah threw her bag on the kitchen counter and turned to face Jamie. "Sit." She indicated a seat at the island in the kitchen.

Reluctantly Jamie sat, keeping silent.

"So," Sarah said.

"So what, Mum?" Jamie asked her defiantly.

"Did I just find out you are gay tonight?"

Jamie tried to find the right words but knew it would take longer to think about it.

"I asked you a damn question." Sarah slapped her hand on the counter.

"Would it be the end of the world?" Jamie snapped back. "I was going to tell you soon, but I had to know what I was going to say."

"Something along the lines of, 'Hey, Mum, guess what? I'm gay.'"

Jamie was actually a bit scared. His mum had lit a fuse and was about to take off into space.

"You think it would have been that easy? Look at your reaction now."

Sarah was pacing, her high heels clacking on the wooden floor. Jamie continued to sit very still. His mum had never hit him. Was there a first time for everything?

"Mum," he started again. "I wanted to tell you, just us, it was…"

"Yeah, but instead of that," she said sourly, "I find out in front of Danny and his dad. You have ANY idea how humiliating that was for me?" She spat the word ANY out as though it was a bad taste in her mouth.

"That wasn't the plan. I had no idea you were out with his dad." Jamie could feel his voice rising and he wanted to keep this together. Let his mum lose her shit. She would be the one having to apologise later.

Sarah swung round. "What? So, this is my fault now?"

"No, Mum, I didn't say that. I just meant that events overtook themselves." Jamie gave out a sob. He hadn't meant that to happen either. How was he going to make this right? He felt walking out to his room would be the best thing to do, let her cool down. He also knew if he got up, she would tell him to sit back down.

Sarah was still pacing about.

Jamie continued. "You know what, Mum, when Danny told his dad last weekend, his dad gave him a big hug and said he loved him."

Total. Silence.

Had he hit a nerve?

"Give me your phone." Sarah held out her hand.

"What?" Jamie looked confused. "Are you going to go through my messages?"

"Should I? What will I find?" She still had her hand outstretched. "I have no intention of going through your phone but I don't want you contacting Danny."

Jamie felt his blood beginning to boil. "You can't be serious."

Sarah laughed. "Deadly. Hand it over." She was now clicking her fingers.

"Mum, I am nearly seventeen. We are not in school now; this is ridiculous. Can we not talk about this?"

"We need to have some space."

"I need to check if Danny is OK. I was a total shit back there. I said nothing. I didn't run after him. He's alone."

"Not your problem. Give me your fucking phone. NOW!"

Jamie had never seen his mum like this. They had rowed before. Stupid things. Surely this was a stupid thing. Why was she kicking off at him for being gay? Jamie had had doubts about telling her, but he had also thought it would be a minor glitch, then she would be fine.

Jamie decided he just needed to get out of the kitchen, retreat to anywhere his mum was not. He fished out his phone and slid it across the table.

"I can't believe this, Mum."

"Neither can I, Jamie."

Jamie looked confused as he was not even sure what she couldn't believe. That he was gay? He didn't lie about it. Nobody else knew. She wasn't the last one to find out. He got up.

"Did I say you could leave?"

"You won't talk to me about it so I'm going to my room. Maybe we can both calm down."

"There's nothing to talk about." Sarah took the phone off the counter.

"I'm not letting you take Danny away from me." Jamie was defiant.

Sarah laughed but Jamie was gone.

So, there we have it, that's what went down at Jamie's. I wasn't privy to any of that; maybe just as well. I would have wanted to send the SAS in. Little did I know that something much better than the SAS was about to take control.

"So, you haven't seen or heard from him at all?" Dad asks as I relay the news about Jamie.

"No. Katie did wonder if they had done a runner back to Basingstoke but his mum was in school today."

"Maybe couldn't face it?"

My shoulders sag, again. "But surely a text just saying 'hi' wouldn't have killed him?" I've now stopped wanting him to say sorry, because having thought things through, it really wasn't his fault. If I knew where he lived, I would probably be on the verge of going round to try and rescue him from the cellar.

Dad is thoughtful for a bit.

We have just finished tea.

It's 6:48pm. I don't like 24-hour clocks. 18:48 doesn't cut it for me as a time.

I notice him looking at the clock too.

I had a questioning look on my face.

"I've left my bloody folder in Mick's car. I'll text and see if he's in, I can go pick it up. I've got work to do this weekend. Shit!"

I clear the table as he is busy texting. After a few moments his phone pings.

"Yes, it's there. He has conveniently had a glass of wine so I'll have to go round. You going to be alright?"

"I'm going to be fine, Dad. I'm not going to climb on the garage roof and throw myself off." I gave him a 'what the actual freak?' look. "Go get your folder. I'll pick us out a slasher movie for later. Bridget Jones won't cut it tonight."

Dad picks his keys up and is gone.

CHAPTER 18
Dad

Now, normally you'd have to wait until Dad gets back with his folder to find out this bit of the story because after all, it is my tale, and I'm the narrator. However, I'm going to be like *The Little Bluebird* and allow Dad to have his five minutes of fame and take over the story; two people writing my story. I will, however, be warning him that any deviation from the actual story for his own personal gain or dramatic effect will be overruled. I'm not giving him total free rein. He will not be telling the story in the first person.

Here goes.

Dad leaves in the car to retrieve his folder from Mick, but he turns left at the bottom of the road instead of right, and after ten minutes comes to a stop outside a large semi-detached Victorian villa in the posh end of town. The drive is paved in red sets and a red Mercedes C-class is parked on it neatly. The borders could use some work and a large hedge along the front of the property is in need of attention.

Dad walks up to the front door, knocks, and waits.

The door opens and Sarah-Sally Walton-Waycross-Burton

opens the door with a slightly startled look on her face.

"Hello, Charlie," she eventually manages.

Dad gives a half smile. "I have a very heartbroken boy at home. Can we please try and sort out how to make things good again?"

Go, Dad!

It almost seems as though Charlie isn't going to be asked in, but Sarah eventually backs against the door and waves him in.

Charlie took in the original features of the spacious hall, the parquet tiling, the picture rail and stained-glass windows above the door. *Very smart. Must have a bit of money*, he thinks.

Sarah leads the way into the large kitchen at the end of the hall. Or do you call halls in Victorian villas 'passages'?

The kitchen has obviously been modernised and now sports a large island unit fairly cluttered with stuff, a bowl of fruit, one of flowers, a stack of papers, Sarah's handbag, and then Dad spots a wicker basket with a sign saying 'confiscated items', and recognises Jamie's very distinctive black and silver metal-cased mobile phone sitting in the bottom of it.

Sarah moves to put the island between her and Charlie and stands with the palms of her hands flat on the surface. She looks composed. "So, is your son in love with my son? Is that what you want to talk to me about?" she asks defensively.

Charlie holds his hands up. He had rehearsed what he felt he should say, but now he wasn't sure. He didn't want to antagonise Sarah, but equally he felt the boys should have a voice. They were approaching seventeen, after all.

"I want Danny to be happy above all else. Surely you want the same for Jamie?"

"What if I'm not happy about all this, though. Do I not get a say?"

"We have to remember they are young adults," Charlie started but was cut off.

"That may well be the truth but while Jamie is living under my roof, my rules apply." Sarah slapped the work surface with her palm.

"I think we have to look at this with a bit more sensitivity. If I lost Danny because I told him how to run his life, I'd be distraught. It's just me and him now. You must feel like that too? Just you and Jamie." Charlie stands tall. He's not going to be bullied by anyone.

"Where else is he going to go? He has to live here."

"You're not worried he would go back to his dad?"

Hit a nerve there.

"How dare you suggest that? You know nothing about my husband."

"I'm not saying I do know anything about Jamie's dad, but he is just that, and if he finds out there is friction between you two, he could easily use that as a bargaining tool to get Jamie to go and live with him."

Sarah paces behind her island fortress. "I know Jamie wouldn't do that. He hates him as much as I do."

"OK, but wouldn't you rather know that Jamie and Danny are safe either here or at my house rather than wondering where they are, roaming about because we won't let them meet?"

"What are you suggesting?" This is a different woman to the one Charlie had dated just yesterday.

"I mean, if we stop them meeting and they do think a lot about each other, they will find a way to see each other, and I for one do not want Danny in some disused electrical substation on a shitty night because I didn't let them be at home." Charlie is on the verge of losing it and has to rein himself back in. "Sarah, my kid is the most important thing in my life, as Jamie should be in yours, and this last week or so he has been the happiest I have ever seen him, and that's what I want for him. I also think Jamie is a damn fine young man. He is polite and courteous and I would be happy for them both to hang out together."

"But, that's just it, they wouldn't just be hanging out, would they?"

"Why is that such a big issue?"

"If you're happy for your son to be screwing some other boy while you watch TV downstairs then I'm happy for you to do that. I have a few more morals than that."

Charlie reckons that if there had been an ornament to hand, she would have picked it up and thrown it.

"I've got my morals, Sarah. I've also got common sense. What good is it going to do to alienate everyone? Let's spread some happiness."

"It's not the 1960s, Charlie. Flower power and drugs and..." She cuts herself off, not really knowing where she's going with this.

"It's so much harder to be angry, but I don't see why we are being angry. Danny is a changed kid since he met Jamie. I feel so happy for him but tonight he is a wreck. I want a happy Danny back."

Sarah gives a big sigh.

"So, all these names and the fact you teach Danny, but didn't allow him to know you were Jamie's mum – that's OK? Why all the secrecy?" Charlie reaches over and picks Jamie's phone up out of the basket. "And what the hell is this? I know this happens in school but you're stopping him having any contact with the outside world? Is he locked in his bedroom?"

"I think I'd like you to leave, Charlie." Sarah walks round and makes her way to the passage door.

"Sarah, come on. Okay, I'm sorry, but we can't leave this like this."

Sarah swings around. "Jamie couldn't even tell me he is gay. He told you though. Have you any idea how that makes me feel?"

"He didn't tell me. He told Danny. And, you know what, Sarah? He was terrified about telling you." Charlie softens his voice. "He wanted to tell you. He was going to tell you. He was frightened how you might react." He throws his arms open. "Maybe he had right to be worried about how to tell you."

Sarah's shoulders sag a little and Charlie notices this. "Come on, Sarah, really, how awful is this? We have two amazing kids. They have both been through such a lot recently and we should be supporting them."

Sarah supports herself on a high stool at the island. It looks as though she's deep in thought. Is she about to crumble?

Charlie thought, *Gotta keep this up. I'll break her!*

"I thought we were doing OK, too? I really enjoyed last night. Let's not fight."

Sarah sits quietly. Is she about to blast off into space again, or collapse in a heap and fall into Charlie's arms?

Charlie sits on the stool next to her. "Is the gay thing the issue?" he asks quietly.

"It's everything, Charlie," her voice cracks. "I thought we were coming for a fresh start."

"You have, but this can all be a part of a fresh start. Even if we don't work out, we can still be friends and look out for the boys. Ask yourself, had he brought home a nice girl, would we be having this conversation?"

"I had it all planned out. Settle here, get a good job…" She looks up at him. "I always use my maiden name for teaching so that's nothing new and when I found out I would be covering maternity at Jamie's sixth form we discussed it and decided it was best if people didn't know we were mother and son, you know, just in case there were any issues for him, more than me. Maybe I overthought things."

Charlie perches quietly, looking down at his shoes. "Can I tell you something?"

"What?" Sarah asks.

"I had Danny give me fashion advice for our first date. He told me what I should wear and I remember you saying you liked my shirt. I would have worn the wrong one had I organised myself. That's how much I trust him. We look out for each other. He is an amazing kid and I actually dread him going off to uni in a couple of years, but I would never tell him that." Charlie continues. "I suppose seeing him now, going through this phase of his life, telling me he is gay – and by the way I've only known for a week – and meeting Jamie, and being all worried if he is saying the right things and doing the right things, asking for advice, is all another part of his growing up. Yes, I do worry he is moving faster than I would like but I would never hold him back unless of course I did think he was doing something very stupid."

Charlie reaches across and takes Sarah's hand. She lifts her head.

"Why don't we work on this together?" he asks. "Teamwork?" He squeezes her hand.

Sarah gives a sigh. "I've already cocked it all up, though,

haven't I? Jamie hasn't spoken to me all day, and yes, you're right, what mother takes her sixteen-year-old's mobile when he needs to talk to someone about stuff? You are such a good father, Charlie."

"Hey, I don't get it right anywhere near all the time." Charlie smiles and feels the ice may be thawing.

"Jamie has talked about you and Danny."

"Really?"

"Yes, about the history project, about Danny's mum. About you, about how he wished his dad had been more like you. He realises what a good connection you and Danny have."

There's a pause. Charlie feels there's more coming so he keeps quiet.

"I guess maybe I was jealous? I don't have that bond with Jamie. Yes, we get along but I'm cold, Charlie, not the loving, hugging mother I should be. Maybe it's the teacher in me, always on my guard."

"I'm sure he realises it's tough for you. You have moved him from school, from his home and friends, and you are having to manage without your husband here on your own."

Sarah gives Charlie a look.

"I'm not for one moment saying you can't manage, but it's a whole change of life for you both. You do want the best for Jamie, I know you do."

"I do, Charlie. I do want the best for him. He's a good kid. Danny's a good kid too. I nearly lost it in class that day with him, but he was so grown-up about it and made me see I had overstepped the mark."

Charlie looked at Sarah. "What thing in class?"

Of course, I hadn't told Dad because I didn't need him getting upset about Mum.

Sorry, I'm still listening in!

What did you expect?

I need to know when to step in if needed but Dad, you're doing a cracking job so far.

Carry on!

Sarah realises suddenly that Danny hadn't told his dad. "It was just something and nothing that I let take over and I should have dealt with it better. Danny did let rip and he came and found me later and apologised. That takes a special person to do that, Charlie, and Danny is special."

"OK," Charlie says. "I think. He never mentioned any problem in school." Charlie doesn't want to let this new revelation overshadow the real issue here so he moves back to the problem in hand. "So, how are we going to sort this out?"

"I don't know. You're the one with all the answers, maybe you tell me."

"I would never do that, Sarah. We have to decide what's best, but I do think we need to make a decision today. It's too acidic to leave overnight."

"Is Danny blaming me?" Sarah asks.

"No, sadly he is mad at Jamie. I think the lack of communication from him is the big thing. Danny has texted but heard nothing." Charlie indicates the phone in the basket again.

"Crap. Why did I do that?"

"Probably because you thought that was the right thing to do." Charlie shuffles on the stool. "He also thinks Jamie lied to him, because he found out that Jamie knew you were his teacher."

"Will he see Jamie?" Sarah asks.

"I'm sure he will because he still thinks the world of him. He will get over this but maybe we need to move things along a bit."

"OK, what do you suggest?"

"I'd like you to let me take Jamie to ours and have him and Danny talk things through."

Sarah sighs again. "I've got to, haven't I?"

"Not if you still don't want him to see Danny. Everyone has to be comfortable, but I personally think it's the best way to go."

"You are right, Charlie." Sarah stands up. "Shall I call him down?"

Charlie nods and Sarah opens the kitchen door.

Charlie stands up too and catches his reflection in a mirror by the door. *Am I about to pull off the biggest peacetime talks in sixth form this term?* He smiles at himself. *Hope you're proud, Danny, my boy.*

Sarah comes back in. "He's coming down."

Jamie drags himself into the kitchen. He is wearing an oversized baggy jumper and the arms cover his hands. His head is bowed and his shoulders sag.

"Hey, Mr Ross," he says, a little startled. He looks at his mum and back to Charlie. "Am I in more trouble?"

This kid needs a very big hug so that's exactly what my dad does.

"No, Jamie, you're not in any trouble at all," Charlie says, grasping his shoulders. "I've come to see if you will come and talk to Danny, who quite frankly looks as awful as you do." Charlie almost regrets hugging Jamie. His mum should have stepped into the role.

"I don't think he will want to talk to me," Jamie says, distraught. "I haven't been much of a friend, let alone a boyfriend."

"You'd be surprised."

Sarah finally makes a gesture. Removing the phone out of the basket, she hands it to Jamie. "I shouldn't have taken this off you," she says, and I think she means it. "It was childish of me. I'm not in school now." Sarah picks the basket up, flips the lid of the pedal bin and pushes it into it.

Wow, big gesture, Charlie thinks. *Now just give your kid a hug.*

It's not going to happen so Charlie makes a move. "Come on, Jamie, let's get you two talking."

"Are you OK with this, Mum?" Jamie looks a bit worried that he's going behind her back.

"I'm fine with it, honey. I'm sorry I didn't understand." Finally, she pulls him into a hug and rubs his back.

It's all too much for Jamie and he sags into her arms, sobbing.

No words are needed.

"I'll see you in the car," Charlie says to him and pulls the kitchen door closed behind him.

Jamie gets in the car and puts his belt on. He and Dad set off back to ours. Jamie's eyes are red from crying and he's still unsure about this.

"You do know that Danny is back home feeling exactly the same as you, Jamie," Dad says indicating left at the roundabout.

"I should have gone after him though. He'll think I'm weak and I just stood there, unable to speak."

"It was such a huge thing that happened. You had planned to tell your mum in your own time and all of a sudden, the whole event was thrust upon you. You do know your mum loves you and is supportive of you?" Dad manoeuvres the bend in the road and glances across at Jamie. "Yes, I think she could have handled it slightly differently and I also think she is sorry she didn't, and yes, Danny was pissed off about it all, but we've chatted and he's fine about it all now."

"I never got in touch either." Jamie looks down at his feet.

"That was taken out of your control. It does seem as though we're going to have communication problems, as this isn't the first time." Dad looks across at Jamie and smiles, trying to lighten the mood.

"Are you going to ask Danny if he'll talk to me before I come in?"

"I don't need to. I know Danny; he'll be so pleased to see you."

"What if he isn't though? He may have been thinking about it some more."

"Stop overthinking things. You young folk need to lighten up. I don't remember being so angsty when I was your age. I just went with the flow."

"That's because there was no crappy social media. People talked to each other," Jamie sighs.

Dad turns right at the bottom of our drive.

I hadn't climbed onto the garage roof. I'd gotten a Pepsi and gone and laid on the sofa waiting for Dad to get back. It wasn't video night but I needed a blood, guts, and gore type of movie. Dad probably needed it too. I had chosen The Hills Have Eyes, which is a pretty scary film to most people. Dad and I have watched it before and it's usually one of our go-to films if one of us has been stressed. As I said earlier, a slushy film doesn't cut the mustard in times like this. I had gradually moved about so that I was laid flat on the sofa, my left leg stretched over the arm, my right leg bent at the knee with my foot on the floor, and my head perilously close to hanging over the edge of the sofa.

I heard the front door open, then moved my head lower so I could see Dad come into the kitchen.

"Hey," I say. "Get your folder?"

"What?" Dad says, standing in the doorway. "Oh, right, no, I hopefully got something much better."

I screw my eyes up and look at him upside down. "Eh?"

"Somebody to see you."

I close my eyes. "Don't think I can do anyone. It's not Katie, is it?" I raise my voice to carry through to the hall. "Sorry, Katie, just not up to it."

"Not Katie," Dad says and ushers Jamie through.

It's one of those 'press the pause button' moments.

Jamie still looks gorgeous, even when upside down, even with puffy red eyes, even with the arms of his sweater way below his hands, even looking so sad. I need him in my life; I want him so desperately in my life.

"Hey," I say.

Perhaps I should organise myself so I am the same way up as he is.

"Hey," Jamie says. "I'm sorry."

I try to turn and stand up then realise I have been lying with my foot over the arm so long it's gone to sleep, and the moment I try to stand my foot gives way and I end up in a heap on the floor.

"Ever the drama queen," Dad sighs.

I give him a look.

Dad holds his hands up and points back over his shoulder. "OK, I have things to do upstairs. Are you going to play nice?"

I'm desperately trying to make my foot work and pins and needles have now taken over the numbness.

Jamie walks over and takes my hand. "Need some help?"

"Yes please," I say.

He guides me back down onto the sofa, probably the safest place to be until I have two fully functioning feet. He sits beside me.

"You been crying?" I ask.

"Might have been," he says quietly.

"Me too," I say just as quietly.

He is still holding my hand.

"I was so upset by my behaviour. I was sure you wouldn't ever want to talk to me again," he says.

"I was upset too, but not because of your behaviour."

Jamie looks at me, puzzled.

"I was upset that you'd done a runner back down south, or somewhere. You hadn't been in touch at all and I was worried because if I didn't get to see you ever again, we would never get to have that kiss."

He leans forward and our foreheads touch.

We are both quiet. I feel if I speak my voice will be all broken up.

"I'm sorry," Jamie says again. "Everything went totally out of control and I felt like I was in some crazy silent movie and I couldn't speak. Then you ran off and I don't know why I didn't run after you. I was about to lose the best thing in my life and I was doing nothing to save it."

"That's what I felt," I tell him. "I sat by the canal until it was dark."

"Oh, Danny," Jamie said, his voice cracking.

Not just me then, I thought.

"Then Dad talked to me and made me understand what had happened. Did your mum take your phone?"

"Yes."

"Did she tell you not to contact me?"

"Yes."

"Is she mad at you?"

"Not anymore," Jamie says. Then after a pause, "Your dad is just so super brilliant."

"Well, I know that," I say, pulling my head back so I can look him in the eyes.

This is now the place in the story where Jamie would have related everything to me, had I not allowed Dad to take over. I think he did pretty well at storytelling and sorting stuff out.

My dad is just so super brilliant.

He's also a cunning fox, but I can forgive him because he brought Jamie back to me.

We are still looking at each other, our faces about a foot apart.

I can feel tension.

I think Jamie feels it now.

"Would it make you less upset if I kissed you?" Jamie asks.

"I've been waiting for that kiss for too long." I smile for the first time all day.

I feel my chest heaving, my breathing becoming more rapid. This really is too stupid for words; we are both nearing seventeen, neither of us has kissed a boy before, you would think we were about to re-split an atom.

I lean in and our noses touch slightly.

I feel his lips on mine.

I shudder slightly, but it's a good feeling.

The last twenty-four hours blur into fog and disappear.

I'm back outside the restaurant, holding Jamie's hand, telling him I've just had the best time of my life. Instead of walking off, we're about to kiss.

I feel a shiver down my spine. All the hairs on my neck stand on end.

The touch of his hand holding mine is amazing.

It is all such simple stuff, yet it is so powerful.

We gently kiss then pull apart.

"Wow," is all I can say.

Jamie is grinning. It's so great to see that smile on his face again. "Yes, that's what I was going to say."

I am melting in his arms.

'Didn't take much,' I hear you exclaim!

You would be just the same if you were here.

I run my hand over his stubbly head, liking how it feels, then, placing my hand behind his head I pull him in for another kiss.

More intense.

Jeez, how could a kiss do this to me?

I'm not ready for this. Everything is whirling about. Does Jamie feel the same? How have I waited all these years to feel this emotion? I'd watched guys kissing each other on my laptop, wishing it was me experiencing it with another boy, but never in my wildest dreams had I thought this is what it was like.

Bobby, my butterfly, flutters in my chest, tingles rush up

and down my spine, my skin feels sparkly where Jamie is stroking my arm and my head is buzzing like bees reaching into every nook and cranny, but in a good way.

I can feel things stirring down below.

What?

How is this happening?

Is this what kissing a boy does to you?

Makes you lose all control of all your bodily functions?

Wow. It's a wicked feeling, though.

Is Jamie feeling the same?

He's now ruffling my hair. He can do anything to my hair.

Our lips find each other's again and I part mine to allow his tongue to run over my lower lip.

I give a slow sigh; that was even better.

"OK?" he asks, taking a breath.

"So OK," I say, "but stop talking."

So, this is my first boy-on-boy kiss.

Wait, no it isn't!

What about drama class?

But that was just acting.

This is my first *proper* boy-on-boy kiss and it feels crazily perfect!

"Dad, can Jamie stay for video night?"

"It's Thursday." Dad looks at me. "It isn't video night."

"I know, but I'd sort of got one set up, and it sort of seems a waste not to watch it." I look across at Jamie. "If you want to, of course. You may not like my choice of video."

It's just gone 8:30pm.

"He can if he feels up to it. Let me check Sarah is OK with it. She may want some time with him on their own, you know, like we did?"

"Oh, yes, I get it." But I am disappointed.

Please say yes, Sarah.

I don't know what Dad is actually suggesting to Sarah but ten minutes later he comes into the living room. "Your mum is fine with you stopping for video night and as it will be pretty late when it's finished, and so I can have a drink during the film, she agreed to my suggestion that maybe if you would like, you can stay over?"

What the actual freak?

I want to scream!

Jamie is going to stay the night?

"It's a school night," I simply say. "I mean, it's a sixth form night."

"We can get him back in time to get ready for school," Dad says. "Just means an earlier start."

There's a bit of an all-round pause.

"I'd take the chance while Sarah is happy with it," Dad adds, raising his eyebrows.

What the hell does that look mean?

Jamie looks at me. "Is that OK?" he asks.

I can't make my mouth form words and spit them out in an orderly fashion so I simply nod my head manically and squeeze his hand.

Dad looks at me. "I'm sure you can loan Jamie some PJs and there's always spare toiletries in the bathroom cupboard."

Jamie and I are beaming.

"OK," Dad says, "let's get this film on the go and maybe you two will stop with the goofy looks." He looks thoughtful for a moment than adds, "Do you two want to have video night on your own? I have seen this film before."

Jamie quickly jumps in. "No way, Mr Ross. Video night is your night." He indicates us both. "I feel honoured to be able to join you and if it's as bad as Danny makes out, I may need some support."

"You won't get any from me, Jamie," Dad says, hands on hips. "If you can't stand the heat, you know where the door is." Then he laughs.

"Told you," I say. "Dad is brutal on video night."

Jamie flops back. "OK, I'll try and be brave."

Somehow this feels wrong all of a sudden. I so want to have Jamie in my life but it feels like I am leaving Dad behind. Friday is our night, our video night. We have never had anyone else join us, yet it had been my idea. Now looking across at Dad on the chair, one leg over the arm, his wine glass in his hand, it looks all wrong. We always sat on the sofa together for video night, we always had the bowl of nibbles just on the table, now we couldn't all reach the bowl. Sometimes I even sat with my feet on his lap and he would place the cushion on top of my feet and balance the bowl on that; a silly thing but it's what we did.

Am I regretting asking Jamie to stay?

Of course not. The look on his face when I asked and then when his mum said that was OK was worth every penny.

Jamie is sitting where Dad would normally have sat. Only our bodies are touching and I am holding his hand. I certainly wouldn't have done that with Dad. Maybe this is moving on. Moving on slowly. Dad looks absolutely fine but I will talk to him afterwards, see how he is feeling. Two years of Friday-night video night is a big thing.

I think Dad reads my look. "You do realise our video night is Friday and that's not going to change? As it's Thursday we can make an exception and have a guest to join us. Its fine," he adds reassuringly.

Maybe he and Sarah will hit it off and they can have their own video night. Jeez, Jamie's mum and my dad! I think I saw a trailer for a new TV show called something like that, although I wouldn't want to go on TV to promote the idea of my dad with anyone else.

Dad and Sarah.

Is that going to work out?

I realise Dad is looking at me. "Earth to Danny!" He laughs.

I jump out of my thoughts. "Sorry, are we ready to go?"

"Ready as ever; the nibbles are nearly all gone. Should have accounted for three mouths, instead of two," Dad says, grabbing a handful of crisps.

I press play and the credits start to roll. I squeeze Jamie's hand a little more tightly and he grins at me.

I'm about to find out just what Jamie thinks of a good scary movie. About three minutes in, in the foothills three scientists are brutally murdered. One has a pickaxe thrust through his back, another has his head split open. I thought every bone in my hand was going to be broken.

"Seriously?" he asks. "Why would they do that?"

Then a box is found and there is an ear in it.

Jamie looks across at me. "Can I change my mind? You are both crazy. Why would you watch this?"

I hope he is joking. I don't want him to release my hand and leave.

Back in the film, the most annoying dad in the world is taking his family on a camping trip that none of them want to go on. It is very clear that things are going to happen. All the tyres on the truck and caravan are blown out and weird people, the result of a scientific experiment, lurk in the shadows.

I pass Jamie a cushion and I kid you not, he does have it at the ready to hide behind.

"What did you say the other option had been for tonight?" he asks as the film finally ends.

"Bridget Jones," I say.

"What was the reason that we didn't watch that?" he asks.

"It just wasn't going to cut it, the state Danny was in earlier. He needed blood, guts, and gore."

"Maybe you need to have your video nights without me in future."

"Lightweight," Dad chortles.

"I'm not going to sleep tonight." Jamie's voice is shaky.

Dad's on his feet, heading for another glass of wine. He punches Jamie on the arm and looks at me. "You'll have to give Jamie a very big safe cuddle in bed." He laughs as he heads to the fridge.

I look at Jamie and he looks at me.

Eyebrows are raised.

I'm going to what?

A big safe cuddle in bed?

In my bed?

Jamie and me?

Jamie raises his eyebrows a little and smiles. "It will be worth watching that slasher movie if I'm going to get a very big safe cuddle," he whispers in my ear.

I always imagined if I was straight, I would ask a girl out at school, we would go bowling, come back to mine and rip each other's clothes off and have wild sex, then she would pull her jeans back on, say it was nice but she has to go.

That would be it.

That's what I've heard guys saying at school.

This doesn't seem to be much like that.

I feel Jamie and I have this amazing connection that requires slow, gentle making out. I haven't even thought about sex. Has Jamie? Does he feel like me? Is he desperate to rip my clothes off, have wild sex and walk away?

I hope not.

Jamie skips off to the loo so I take the opportunity to just double check with Dad that he is happy for Jamie to sleep in my bed. Has he just been larking about, two glasses of wine and all that?

"You're both sensible kids," he starts. "If I say no and you really want to, you will only creep into someone else's bed in the middle of the night." Dad looks at me questioningly.

"If you'd said no, I wouldn't," I tell him.

He pulls me in for a hug. "Actually, I know you're telling the truth. You don't need my permission though."

Jamie walks back in and sees me and Dad hugging. We don't break away just because he's come in. That's the kind of relationship Dad and I have and I really don't think that's how Jamie and his mum are.

Which is sad.

I know what you're thinking. Get in the real world. What family really has the love that we do?

And, you're right. Too many families don't make time for love and spending quality time together. I know that when I do move out and make my own way in life, I will always have time for Dad.

Awkward

Just over an hour later Jamie and I are in my bedroom.

This is my safe space. Dad always knows if the door is shut, I want some time on my own and never once has he come in without knocking and waiting, and only then if he needs something urgent.

The door is shut now, but this time I have a gorgeous boy in here with me and the intention is that we will be sleeping together in my bed.

What is Jamie expecting?

What am I expecting?

I am actually a bit terrified.

My heart is doing a mini rhumba in my chest. Bobby has fled the building, unable to flutter about any longer.

Would a girl and a boy feel like this? I guess not.

What do I know?

I am wandering aimlessly, getting a set of sleep shorts and tee-shirt out of a drawer for Jamie. Does he sleep naked? I usually don't wear a tee-shirt but I will tonight.

Will I?

Should I just, you know?

Oh, jeez!

Jamie seemed to pick up on my anxiety. "Would you rather I sleep in the guest room?" he asks quietly.

I look at him. "No, of course not. I..." I falter. What do I really want?

He takes me in his arms and we hug close. "This is a bit freaky for me," he says, rubbing my back.

"Me too, but why?" I ask him.

I can feel the tension coming from Jamie too, so it's not just me, thank you kindly! I would have been worse if he had been like, 'Okay, let's do this,' gung-ho.

"Are you upset that I don't just want to jump into bed and rock the headboard?"

Maybe he feels me sag a bit. "No, I'm sort of happy that you don't want to do that."

"Thank God," Jamie says. "My heart has been beating out of my chest for the last twenty minutes worried that you were going to..." He trails off.

"Shag you senseless?" I ask.

"Something like that." Jamie pulls in again. "I do want to, I think, but not yet."

I couldn't love this amazing boy any more than I already do.

My heart is pounding, but for a whole different reason now we have got the elephant in the room dealt with.

I feel so much more relaxed, I can't wait to be cuddling up to Jamie.

There's a problem with wearing sleep shorts, especially when you happen to be with a very gorgeous boy! There is no restraint or protection from sudden erection-type problems! I hop straight into bed hoping Jamie hasn't seen my predicament, but chancing upon a quick glance in his direction seems to show he is having the same problem.

Oh my!

What to do?

Jamie sits on the edge of the bed away from me and swings himself in. I want to laugh out loud!

What.

Were.

We.

Like?

A small giggle escapes, unplanned.

Jamie looks across and asks if I'm OK.

"Think so. You? Sorry about the chuckle, I just, well if you could see the pair of us, dodging about getting into bed."

"I was trying to hide my…" Jamie starts, then I see his ears colouring. Maybe he hadn't meant to say that out loud.

"Hey, same problem here," I tell him. "Only difference being I managed to get under the duvet before you saw!"

"You monster." Jamie goes to tickle me. "Yeah, but this feels like, so weird. Is that a bad thing to say?"

"Don't think so." I turn to face him. "I've wanted this, like, forever, to be laid next to another boy. I've fantasised about it a lot." I look him in the eye. "Well, not any other boy. This boy," I say and I trace my finger down the side of his face.

Jamie nods. "I can understand you, although I often thought it would be a girl for me, until you came along."

My heart crashes inside my ribcage. Is Bobby back and all aflutter? Again?

I reach across and put my arm across his chest as Jamie lays next to me. He turns to face me, smiles, then kisses my nose.

I smile back and we kiss. Gently and tenderly. I feel his lips on mine. It doesn't help any in the erection department! I open my lips slightly and let his tongue explore.

Somebody lights a sparkler and it seems to fizz around the inside of my mouth. I closed down on his tongue and feel his tongue against mine.

"Mmm," he says with a mouthful of tongue, "that feels good." He strokes my hair, managing to twist his fingers into the longer part on the top of my head.

What would it feel like if he stroked me somewhere else?

I think it would be very, very easy to lose control.

Jamie pulls me close and I swear I can feel his heart beating through the thin tee-shirt. I can feel his warmth as we have a very big, safe cuddle.

Dad's words, not mine!

Then Jamie does what I was hoping he would do. He runs a hand down over my tummy and ends a few inches away from, well you know where he ends up!

I gasp in pleasure and he hasn't even touched me.

"OK?" he asks.

"I think you should stop."

The smile fades from his face.

"Something inexplicable will happen if you go any further," I smile, "and quite frankly I think I will have no control whatsoever."

The smile returns to his face; I even think there is a bit of a wicked glint in his eye and he moves his hand lower.

Please feel free to use your imagination at this point. I have no control over my thoughts or my actions, whoops!

Writing, currently not an option!

CHAPTER 19
Friday 6th October

There's a gap in the curtains and the sun finds it and shines a strip of light over Jamie's arm as it lays across my chest. I lie still, listening to his gentle rhythmic breathing, and wonder what I've done to feel this happy. I look over to my tall bookshelf where Mum sits on the top and I chat to her when I have stuff going on in my head. I smile and know she would be smiling too, looking down on me entangled with this gorgeous boy.

Jamie stirs and opens his eyes. He smiles and says a simple, "Hey."

I stroke his arm and look into his eyes. "Hey, handsome," I reply. "Your phone has been vibrating."

After a few moments of waking up he reaches across and flips it open. He closes it up. "Mum gently reminding me, her words I might add, that we both have sixth today and it's already 7am."

"It's worth an early start."

"What is?" he asks.

"That thing that you did to me last night." I pull him close.

"Oh, that old thing." He laughs. "Might do it again if you let me."

"You'd better," I say, and prod his arm.

"Ouch."

Dad shouts from outside that it's now twenty past seven and we need to be getting a shift on.

I check my phone as I sit on the edge of the bed. Katie has sent a simple text asking if I am OK. She knew to leave me alone until I got in touch with her but I guess she just needed to know. I reply that I am indeed OK and if she would like to present herself at the crossing, I would have news for her.

Dad has the table laid and cereal and fruit juice already sorted.

"You'll have to stay more often," I say to Jamie. "Don't normally have a spread like this on a morning."

"Take no notice, Jamie, we normally have a Full English but I've run out of time." Dad gestures to Jamie to take a seat. "I've had a text from Mum to say I have to return you by 8am so get cracking."

Seems Sarah is just checking up on Jamie. Is that what it is?

Dad is dropping Jamie off on his way to work and I am heading to the crossing for a Katie meet. We've decided I won't end up with Jamie at his, just in case his mum does want to talk to him on her own before school.

I kiss him gently on the lips and we go our separate ways.

Katie is waiting by the crossing. I have decided to play it cool to start with, so have a fairly bored look on my face. I'm giving nothing away. Pretty naughty of me, I know, but hey, let's have some fun with Katie.

"Have you heard from Jamie?" I think she is hesitant

because obviously the latest news is that we would never see him again, his mum having trailed him back to Basingstoke.

"Er, yes actually," I say.

"And?" she prompts.

"We're OK." I say simply.

"OK, or more than OK? God, Danny, I can't stand it. I can't stand it if you two have broken up before you got started."

"He had video night with us and stayed over." There, I have told her.

"What? Stayed over?" Is that a smile on her face?

I can't help it, my face breaks into a beaming smile. "We are so bloody OK."

But of course, she isn't happy. "I don't remember being asked if he could sleep in my bed." The spare room is in reality Katie's domain; she stays over now and again for a sleepover.

"He didn't sleep in your bed," I say calmly.

You know I told you about someone pressing the pause button for a moment and everything standing still? Well, Katie pulls me to a stop and turns me to face her.

"What is this you are telling me?"

"He didn't sleep in your bed," I confirm.

"You made him sleep on the couch?" But I know her too well. She's playing with me.

"Summerhouse, actually," I throw back at her.

Katie is full on smiling now. "You liar!" she screams. "Did you and he, well, you know."

"Watch out, people are listening, people are stopping to see what the racket is about."

"Do I care?" Katie asks, hugging me. "So, tell me everything, absolutely everything."

"We made him watch The Hills Have Eyes," I say, laughing.

"Baptism of fire. I remember you trying to get me to watch that. That ear in the box, yeuch!" Katie holds her hand to her mouth. "But, forget all that, I want details. I didn't even think you were still talking to each other and now you tell me you ended up in bed together," she said gleefully. "I am so mega happy for you both. I take it everything has worked out then?"

I fill her in about Dad's journey to see Jamie's mum and what transpired. I still think I have the best dad in the world. How many other dads would have tried to resolve a love issue between a boy and his boyfriend? I am still having to pinch myself to believe it.

Katie is trying to form a question. "So, I don't want to ask how it was because that's your business but, well…"

"But you really want to know?" I laugh.

"No, but, no, it's your thing and I'm really happy for you." Katie is sort of jumping around like a toddler.

I look across at her. "We just had the most amazing cuddle and I fell asleep in his arms and then we woke up and the sun was shining through the curtains and it was, well, it was just wonderful." I hug myself at the memory.

"Does Jordan know?" Katie studies my face for a response.

"No, I haven't seen or heard from him. I think he was staying at Mark's. They were having a video game night. You don't think I would have told him anyway? Not before you. I wouldn't do that to you twice in one week."

"Just checking." Katie loops her arm through mine and we head off again. "Got you trained right, haven't I?"

I give a grin but didn't need to reply.

OK, ready for this?

Are you ready?

My boyfriend, yes you heard right, my boyfriend, is already draped over a chair in the common room when we arrive. I could literally eat him up. Katie is so going to get sick of me in a very short time, I can tell you. I stroke his arm casually, but carefully so no-one sees, as we reach him. He smiles.

"Hey, superstar," he says.

"I'm going to buy a new notebook," Katie says.

I look at her, puzzled.

"So that I can record how many terms of affection you two are going to throw at each other before term ends."

"Ha," I say, but I'm loving it.

"Everything OK?" I ask him, in a quiet voice.

"Yeah, but you may not like what I have to ask you."

How bad can it be? I wondered. "Go on then, ask away." I perch on the arm of his chair. Were we starting to be a bit obvious?

"Mum is issuing an invite to tea," Jamie tells me.

"OK," I say hesitantly.

"Tonight."

"Ooh, OK, well I'm sure that's fine, isn't it?"

"It won't be pizza, or lasagne, or anything with chips."

"If you keep saying food items you are going to run out of things to list," I say to Jamie. "But I like beetroot."

"Don't joke," he warns. "You don't have to say yes."

"How could I say no?" I reply as we head off to maths. "Your mum has made a huge effort for us and I think, I hope, she is wanting to make things OK. Is that how you see it?"

"Yeah, I suppose. I'm sure she's not going to abduct you and drug us, then we both wake up in an institute of correctional therapy."

"Now you're scaring me."

"Just want to show you all the possible options." Jamie holds the door open for me. Is there time to run away again?

Dad thinks it is a good idea too. He agrees with Jamie that Sarah is making an effort and we should encourage it.

"She did allow Jamie to sleep over last night so that was huge in itself and I think if she is now inviting you over, that has to be seen as a good move too."

"I just still feel a bit weird that my boyfriend's mum is also my English teacher, and she is dating my dad."

"Hmm," Dad says. Nothing else to say, really.

So, what to wear for tea with your boyfriend's mum?

I had asked Jamie and he said to just be myself.

And so, I put on clean skinny jeans, a short-sleeved shirt and my rust-coloured cord jacket. Cherry-red DMs, but as I pull them on, I think, *Should I just wear trainers?* I wonder if there is a shoe policy in Jamie's house. Here we have wood floors throughout and Mum always said our house was our home, not a show-house, and therefore unless we were caked in mud, we didn't remove shoes while downstairs. I keep my boots on and decide I will take a chance.

"Have fun," Dad calls as I say a cheery farewell.

"Will you be OK on your own?" I ask him.

"No, I'm going upstairs to have a good cry." Dad gives me a look. "I'll be fine."

I have decided to walk; it's just under a mile and the air will clear my head and I can think things through. Maybe that's not a good idea, actually, what with my paranoia and the like. Although I can't think of anything to kick that off. I think, so long as Jamie and I are OK we can weather any storm.

Talking of storms, it starts to rain as I get to the midway point and a hundred metres or so further on the heavens open.

Really?

I dash into a bus shelter and do just that, shelter. The bus comes but I wave him on; it's the wrong one anyway. I have no hat and my jacket has no hood. I hear you tutting. What teenager doesn't wear a hoodie? Well today, I'm not wearing one. The rain is not easing, and as I look at my watch, I realise I'm going to be late if I don't make a move. I pull my collar up and make a dash for it. I do run faster than I have for a while and frankly I should just walk. I don't honestly think I can get any wetter. I can feel it running down inside my shirt. My feet are now wet, but I think that's just the effort of me running and splashing water up. I am the only fool out in it.

I round the corner and see Jamie's house. I run up the path and get under the porch, ring the bell and start shaking rain from my hair, which by now will be looking dreadful, I imagine.

Jamie pulls the door open and gives a gasp. "What happened to you?"

I looked up to the sky. "You really have to ask?"

"Did your dad not bring you?"

Any more pointless questions and I am going to pull Jamie out into the rain and get him soaked too.

"I think you need a towel," he says as he goes in.

Truly, if I could have grabbed his arm, he would have been

out in it by now!

I stand dripping on the doormat.

Sarah wanders through from the kitchen and takes one look at me. "Interesting look, Danny," she says, but gives a smile so I feel a bit better. "You should have phoned. I could have picked you up."

OK, so why had I not thought of that? "Raining," I say.

"Seriously?" she asks.

"Jamie has gone to get towels," I try to explain as he comes bounding down the stairs.

"I think you may need more than a towel. You look soaked to the skin." Sarah looks at Jamie. "Let's get Danny some clothes. You must have some joggers he can borrow."

"Sure," Jamie sniggers and dashes off back upstairs. For a moment I think I'm in Jordan's house, the way he bounds down the stairs then back up again.

"I'll let you get sorted, Danny. I'm sure I have things to attend to." Sarah disappears and closes the kitchen door.

Jamie is back with grey joggers and a tee-shirt, and a pair of socks.

"Do you need help getting out of those wet clothes?" he asks with a wicked grin.

"Yeah, shall I go get your mum?"

Jamie's smile turns into a grimace. "Spoiled it now."

"I'm sorry, hon, will a swift kiss make things better?"

"It will be a start." Jamie is on me like a rash.

"Steady," I say, still dripping. "What if—" His kiss stifles my question.

After a weird ten minutes standing on a square of coconut matting removing first my boots and socks, then towelling my hair dry, then removing my shirt, I'm all but ready to try and take my skinny jeans off.

OK, I hear you all!

Big intake of breath. Been there, done that, tried to remove skinny jeans that are stuck to my skin like glue.

And these are so stuck.

"Maybe I should just sit in them?" I ask.

"You will catch pneumonia." Jamie looks at me and I see he is trying not to laugh.

"It's not funny." I scowl.

"It is though," Jamie says. "I bet you would be uncontrollable had it been me."

I purse my lips. "OK, got me in one. The only way these are coming off is if I sit on the floor and you pull them off."

"I can do that." Jamie is eager to make a start.

"But your mum." I indicate the kitchen door. "I need to be on my best behaviour and make a good impression."

Sarah calls from behind the door. "You're not very quiet, the pair of you. I promise I won't come out until you have got his trousers off, Jamie."

My eyes are wide. "Holy shit," I whisper. "I didn't realise I was being so loud."

"You were a bit." Jamie is roaring with laughter. "Sit on the bloody floor, you idiot."

We are by now so cracked up that it's even more difficult to get my jeans off, but after a lot of shuffling the offending articles are off. I am towelled with help from Jamie, which by the way really does not help. Even in my distressed state I cannot avoid the obvious happening. I also think Jamie is paying rather too much attention to certain areas of my body with the damn towel!

Keep up!!

Oops, wrong choice of words.

Eventually I am dressed. "I may need a few minutes," I say, looking down at the joggers.

"Only a few minutes?"

If it isn't for the fact that I am trying my hardest to make a good impression this would all have been hilarious.

After what seems like an age since I arrived, and yes, you guessed it, it has stopped raining and the sun has returned, we make an entrance into the kitchen. I feel a bit like an extra in an episode of Friends and expect there to be rapturous applause as I, an unknown American actor, make my entrance.

Sarah turns and smiles. "Well, you look a little less drowned, Danny."

I'm sure we all think that was probably quite a good icebreaker but no-one says it.

Jamie heads to the fridge and returns with two cans of Pepsi.

Something actually smells quite appetising; I was expecting something to do with vegetables and strange herbs and things. There is a smell of garlic too.

"Do you need me to do anything, Mum?" Jamie asks, seeing the kitchen table isn't set.

"No, all good, I thought we'd eat in the dining room."

This is obviously a surprise by the look on Jamie's face.

"OK," he says. "Shall we just chill in the sitting room for a bit then?" He seems a bit ill at ease. There is a strange atmosphere and I feel Sarah is trying too hard. It doesn't feel natural like at home. Everyone would have just been sitting round as Dad cooked, throwing lively banter around, getting drinks, laying the table, everyone mucking in, but I have to let her get on so I squeeze Jamie's hand and nod towards the sitting room.

Jamie's house certainly has that feminine touch to it, which again surprises me a bit, knowing his mum; lots of chintz but tastefully done. That's probably my gay gene coming out!

I'm not saying our house hasn't got the feminine touch because a lot of what Mum's done is still very evident.

Jamie opens the door. A lovely room with the original fireplace, bay window, huge swathe of curtains, big bookcase full of books. I wonder if there's anything Sarah has written, remembering a lit bit evilly that she is now not an author. There are two dogs at either end of the mantle-shelf and a dark wood mirror above the fireplace. I look in the mirror and see a reverse picture on the back wall certainly of Sarah, but with a boy with a head of curls. It's obviously a posed picture, probably professionally taken as the boy is sat on the floor with bare feet looking relaxed. I turn to look at it properly.

It is Sarah, looking happy in a flowing red skirt and white chemise and as I go closer, I realise it's Jamie.

I look at Jamie and he gives me a questioning look.

"This is obviously you." I point at the picture.

"Oh, yes, ah," he says.

"When was it done?" I ask, falling in love with him all over again. He looks relaxed, sexy, the top two buttons of his shirt open, sat on the floor with one leg bent at the knee.

"Through the summer, before we moved up here."

"But, but," I reach out to touch the picture, "what happened to your hair?"

"What? Now, you mean?"

"Well obviously," I say. "Jeez, if you had turned up at sixth with that head of hair, I would have certainly asked you out a lot faster. You look stunning." His curls fell over his left eye and to his collar, and looked so natural.

"I wanted a change from the old me. New start and all that."

I go to him and rub his head. "Would you grow them back?"

"Is that a general question or a request?" He smiles at me.

"Well," I start, "I can't really request you to do it."

"Yes, you can." He puts his arm around my waist and pulls me in. "I'd do anything for you." He kisses me.

"Stop," I gasp. "Remember I'm in joggers!"

Jamie laughs and kisses me again.

Sarah calls us through for tea. There are connecting sliding doors from the sitting room to the dining room and we go through.

"Wow," Jamie says. "This all looks amazing, Mum."

Sarah smiles. "I wanted to make an effort."

Good for you, Sarah, I think to myself.

I begin to wonder if Jamie was lying again, as a lasagne is steaming away on a large table mat and a huge basket of bread is oozing buttery garlic. My stomach rumbles. Where was the butternut salad or nut and herb surprise?

We take our places and Sarah dishes out. I can't resist asking her about the picture.

"So, Sarah, how did you feel when Jamie cut his curls off?"

Sarah looks up. "I was devastated, Danny. A lot of people would kill for curls but he came home one day and it was all gone. I cried all night."

"If both of you are at all interested, I've decided to grow them back," Jamie comments as he takes his plate of food from his mum.

Sarah beams. "Really?"

"Yep," he says, and looks at me as if to say, 'I'm doing it for Danny.'

Heart.

Beating.

Rapidly.

Totally.

In.

Love!

"Sarah," I say, bringing myself back down to earth, "this is amazing!"

"Mum, why don't we have this more often? It's truly scrummy," Jamie confirms.

"Well, maybe like you and your hair, it's time I made some changes. I hate butternut squash!" she laughs.

It is so like Dad's; I want to ask Sarah if she got the recipe from him but decide against it. I have to admit I was worried about being served something I wouldn't even recognise, let alone like.

Ice, well and truly broken.

I see a different side to Sarah from that night outside the restaurant and I think I owe it all to Dad. What would have happened if he hadn't been dating her? Would he have gone to see her, not knowing her?

After eating, Sarah says she's going to clear up but I say to her, "Usually whoever cooks gets let off washing-up duties, so Sarah, with your permission, Jamie and I will go clear up."

I pull Jamie up, who looks a bit reluctant, but I give him the glad eye and he warms to the idea.

"I can't let you do that, Danny; you are our guest."

Jamie pipes up. "Hey, I had to help wash up at Danny's so it's only fair he helps here."

Sarah gives him a look. "OH, I have loads of marking to do. I may go up to the study and get on with that."

I really didn't want her to do that. Dad would have hung around while the gang were there, all chilling together. But I am coming to realise Sarah is not as relaxed as my little family are. I think even Gramps is way cooler that her.

We part at the stairs and Jamie and I go into the kitchen to face the devastation.

I survey the pots and pans. "Crikey, now I know why you weren't keen to do this." I squeeze his tiny ass and smile at him.

It does the trick.

He smiles back. "Don't you start any messing around in my kitchen, young man. We have work to do."

I hug him tight and plant kisses all over his mouth.

He looks into my eyes. "I thought you were worried on the trouser front."

"I was," I say, looking down. "Shit, I am!"

Jamie reaches down.

"Do not under any circumstances touch me. Do you want to wash or dry?"

"I did have other plans." He has that wicked look in his eye.

"Er, that would be very nice, yeah, but we have work to do."

"Spoilsport," he says, giving me a playful squeeze before retiring to the sink.

Oh, why did he have to do that? I restrain myself from pulling him back to me and making out right there in the kitchen of my English teacher. I look down again; that did the trick!

I am sitting in Sarah's car; Jamie and I have said our goodbyes and she has insisted on driving me home as it is raining again. I have my wet clothes and boots in a bag and am still wearing Jamie's joggers and a tee-shirt, and I borrowed a pair of his trainers, which I said I will return tomorrow but as he thinks I look way too cute in them, I may just keep them.

Sarah pulls the car out onto the road; it's only a mile, so only about three minutes probably, but I feel I ought to say something, other than thank her for the meal, which I do first.

"Thanks, about being, you know, OK about Jamie and me," I start.

"I'm not your English teacher tonight so I won't say you should have said 'Jamie and I'."

"Whoops, sorry," I say.

"I am truly fine, Danny. I know I freaked out a bit to start with and I heard everything about your dad and the way he handled you coming out, and I wish I could have been like him. I actually think you are good together. I was so worried about Jamie not fitting in up here but he seems fine."

"I know people are probably going to find out you are Jamie's mum now. That's not going to be a problem, is it?" I ask her, knowing I had told Katie and she had told Mel and Sam, so I'm sure word would be spreading.

"We will deal with that, Danny. I don't actually teach Jamie so it's not a problem in that I could be biased towards him, and you're both old enough to fight any battles that may cause."

Sarah swung the car into our drive.

"However, that doesn't mean I'll be giving you special treatment either." She smiles at me. "Although I don't think I will need to as you do seem to be managing OK without any help." I think she is referring to *The Little Bluebird*.

"I wouldn't expect it any other way." I unclip my belt. "Thanks for the lift home, saves me having two sets of clothes to wash and dry."

Sarah touches my arm and simply says that I am welcome.

Dad eyes me up as I'm emptying the bag of clothes ready to go in the machine. "Do I need to ask what's happening here?"

"Got soaked in the rain going to Jamie's," I say, opening the door.

"I did wonder. The rain started here about ten minutes after you had left."

"Anything else to go in?" I ask, seeing I was way off a full load.

"I'll go see in a minute." Dad is hanging about.

"You can ask, you know," I say to him.

"Ask what?" He is looking sheepish.

"How it went."

"Oh, yeah, right. How did it go?"

"It was fine." I look at him.

"Just fine?"

"Did Sarah get your lasagne recipe from you?" I ask him.

"Er, she might have done."

"I knew it, but she did it really well and the garlic bread

she bought was probably a tiny bit better than the stuff we get."

Dad gives a sharp intake of breath. "Well, you know what? You can go buy some of it next time and I'll let you know if it is." He punches me playfully on the arm and before he goes off in search of clothes to wash gives me a parting salvo. "Never thought I'd see you in joggers."

I moan. "I know, I couldn't say no. Jamie was so kind to let me have these but I think I'll go find some jeans." I am not, and never have been into joggers, and it's not just the evident problem that arises when I get turned on by some gorgeous boy, and, oh shit, it's happening again, just thinking about him.

Stop!

CHAPTER 20
Saturday 7th October

My phone pings.

"Loverboy, I expect," Katie says.

She is not wrong.

Jamie

Hi, how's the decorating going x

Me

Slowly x

Katie here, twenty questions and all that!

Jamie

Glad I'm not there lol

Me

Wish you were, missing you x

Jamie

Yeah, me too

"Come on," says Katie. "You can chat later once we're done."

Me

Gotta go. Queen B needs my sorry ass in the summerhouse x

Jamie

Okay, go pin things up. Chat later x

Me

X

"How hard can it be to put up a 'Happy Birthday' sign?" Katie huffs. "It's still not straight."

"Maybe we just make it even more lopsided and say that was the plan." I have my head slightly tilted, looking at the wonky sign.

"You think?"

I don't know whether that meant, 'OK, let's do it,' or, 'What on earth do you mean? We have to get it straight.'

I'm excited to see Gramps again tomorrow when he comes to celebrate his birthday with us. Jamie is going to be here too, as well as Katie and Jordan, and Dad tells me that George and Avril, a couple Gramps plays bowls with are going to come too, which will even out the age profile. They live just round the corner from us so, as Gramps says, 'they can have some champagne and totter back down the road.' A shame we can't have champagne; it feels like more than just a celebration of Gramps' birthday.

"That's better," Katie says, stepping back down from the stool and admiring her work. "Thanks for your help, by the way," she adds sarcastically.

"You are more than welcome." I bow low.

"I'm joking."

"So am I." And we both laugh.

CHAPTER 21

Sunday 8th October

Jamie and I have been texting each other. I'm lying in bed waiting for Dad to shout up to say I need to be up, about, and helping. Jamie is telling me about his mum and that they had a really good evening chatting. It would probably have been so much easier for me to ring him, or even dash over and get the lowdown, but I knew if I went over I wouldn't want to leave him, even though we would be seeing each other this afternoon. I'm sure we would get chance to chat later after the party.

"Danny!" Dad calls.

Told you!

"Coming, Dad!" I shout back.

Jordan is lounging on the sofa when I get down ten minutes later. I pull a questioning face at him.

"I thought you said to come this morning and help," he says. "Did you not say that?"

"I don't remember saying that but it's been a bit of a week."

"Yeah, your dad was telling me that you and Jamie have made up but I got no details."

"Blimey, I can't do right for doing wrong. The other day I was letting stuff slip and getting into bother. Now I'm keeping schtum and I'm in bother again." Dad is tidying in his full-on Dad fashion. A lot of stuff seems to be being put into cupboards randomly.

"Don't put my homework in there, Dad," I say as I see him push my books into the dresser drawer. "I'll never find them." I went to retrieve my English work.

He tsked. I swear, he tsked!

"So, any details going begging?" Jordan asks from his place on the sofa.

Dad and I both look at him.

"Help us put stuff in cupboards then we can have a catch-up."

"Oh, that sounds right up my street. I can grab stuff and shove it in cupboards no bother, but as you say, you'll be looking for it in weeks to come." He leaps up and grabs a magazine and looks around for somewhere to put it. Probably going under the sofa cushion.

"On second thoughts," Dad starts, "you two go and chill in the summerhouse for a bit and I'll do this."

Jordan winks at me. "Works every time," he whispers.

"I'm still getting my head round the fact that Jamie's mum is your English teacher and has three different names, and Jamie never mentioned any of this." Jordan has bagged the sofa in the summerhouse and is sprawled catlike along its length.

"To be fair, it was eating him up and he nearly said something when I told him about the events in class that day when I walked out." I sigh. So much has happened in such a short space of time.

"I so wish I had been in your class that day. I cannot imagine you doing that. Mr Normal Guy walking out of class."

"To be honest, I regretted it the moment I did it. Luckily it all turned out OK."

"And is your dad still going out with her?"

"I'm not sure if you would call it 'going out', but yes, they seem to be planning something else. He was just mega amazing when he went to see her. I knew nothing about it until he walked in with Jamie in tow like a lost sheep."

"Aw, so cute." Jordan flips his trainers off. He is settling in.

"He looked," I start, "well, he just looked gorgeous, even with his huge baggy jumper and tear-stained face." I remember the moment vividly.

Jordan turns to face me. "So, is Jamie the one?"

"Could be," I say, "and the good thing is I didn't have to buy any clothes to catch him."

"Oh, come on, I didn't really have to buy any clothes." Jordan stops.

"And you had your haircut. You went to town for Briony."

"She's worth it." Jordan looks starry-eyed.

"And, talking of hair," I start, "I saw this big, framed picture of Jamie at his on Friday and he had long curly hair. He's going to grow it again."

"No way," Jordan says.

"Yes way. If he could look any cuter than he does now then it's in that picture."

"I hope Katie is OK with all the love going on around her."

"Katie is fine with all her boys getting loved up." A voice comes from outside. We spin around and Katie is there. Did I ask her round too, to help? I'm surprised Dad didn't collar her. She would have sorted out the kitchen and put things where they belonged too!

"Hey," we both chorus.

"I heard there was a party," Katie says. She has a drink in her hand.

"Not for, like, hours yet," I say, wishing Jamie were here too. We hadn't hung out with Jordan and Katie as a couple yet.

"Where's Jamie?" Katie asks, sensing what I'm thinking.

"I told him 2pm, I didn't think everyone was turning up early. I'm sure Dad told Gramps 2pm."

"Ping him and get him to come over now," Jordan says.

"He might be busy," I say.

"Won't know unless you try him." Katie looks mischievous.

I ping Jamie.

Jamie

Unfair!

Me

What do you mean?

Jamie

I thought you said 2?

Me

I thought it was but K and J here now

We can all hang in the summerhouse

Jamie

I'm walking along the canal with Mum

Thought I'd show her somewhere outside the four walls

The look on my face must have said it all.

Katie looks at me. "Everything OK?"

"Fine," I say.

Is this what love is all about? Feeling so desperate for him to be here but he's not? I need to get a grip. We do have separate lives and have to do other stuff. I guess it's all just too new at the moment.

Jamie

Mum says we can turn round

I can be at yours in about an hour

Me

I feel awful now

You're having quality time

Jamie

Rather spend it with you though x

Me

I'll be happy to see you whenever you get here

Don't spoil time with your mum

Jamie

Ok. C U soon xx

"Well?" Katie asks.

"He's out with his mum, he will be here in an hour or so."

"Brill."

Why is a tiny bit of paranoia creeping back in? He didn't sound pissed off. I should have thought about it and asked him to come over this morning.

Katie senses me heading off so squeezes my arm. I smile back at her.

Dad is at the door. "Did anyone think to pick the cake up?"

I jump up. "I thought you were getting it last night?"

"No, I thought you were." Dad sags.

"Come on, young people." Katie leads the way and as usual we all follow. Going for the cake takes my mind off being stupid. Like, what am I worrying about?

Just over an hour later there's a knock at the door and I see a goofy, lopsided smile staring at me through the glass. My heart melts. All is well in Danny World again.

"Hey," Jamie says breathlessly. I don't think he is out of breath; he is just being all sexy.

And it's working.

Working a treat. Damn you, you sexy gorgeous boy!

We hug on the step and he whispers in my ear, "This has been the longest time since I saw you last."

"Same here." I rub his back, still hugging.

OK, so you are probably sick of all this by now?

Just ready for some adult conversation?

No? You want more?

You are too easy to please, readers!

Gramps is on his way with George and Avril, three septuagenarians, so we will have lots of adults, probably talking about adult things. Not adult in that way! I have met Avril before but not George. Could be lots of bowling terminology and while I have been bowling before in a bowling alley, I have not encountered crown green bowling. I can tell you are impressed I know what it's called.

I'm hanging around for them to arrive. Jamie, Katie, and Jordan are sitting under a big umbrella near the summerhouse. It is ridiculously warm for October but that's great because it means we can all hang in the garden. I know Dad worries that Gramps and his friends are getting on a bit, although he would never dare say that, and they may be feeling the cold.

I open the door as the bell sounds. No goofy smile coming at me. Just Gramps who is looking super dapper, as ever. He's in jeans and trendy tan trainers with white soles. I kid you not, he can so carry off this look. How is he seventy? He looks fifty!

"Gramps!" I throw my arms around him.

"Hello, Danny, have you grown since I saw you last?"

"It was only last week, Gramps." I laugh.

"I know, but always a good line to throw out." He turns to George and Avril. "Have you all met?"

Avril steps forward and gives me a hug. "Good to see you again, Danny. I like having a hug so I hope you don't mind?"

"Not at all." I hug her back.

George shakes my hand. "Maybe next time, Danny." He smiles. "I don't think I've met you before, have I?"

"No, I don't think so. I met Avril at a bowls match but you weren't there."

They all step inside and Dad is there now.

"Hello, everyone." He hugs Gramps too and then shakes George by the hand. "Avril, you are looking radiant," he says, giving her a hug too.

"Oh, it's lovely to hear all these compliments," she says. Avril wears a flowing floral dress with a navy jacket with gold buttons, and it looks like she was at the hairdressers this morning.

We go through into the kitchen. I see Gramps looking outside. "Oh, my young folk are here already," he states.

Dad raises his eyes. "Yes, they've been here all day making the place look untidy."

"Dad," I object. "They've been helping."

"So that's what you call it?" He laughs.

Avril sits on one of the sofas and George seems to take her lead and sits next to her.

"What can I get you to drink?" Dad asks. "We do have some sparkle for later but if you fancy a cup of tea for now?"

"A cup of tea would be grand." George speaks for them both.

I leave Dad talking to them and go and put the kettle on. Gramps follows me and looks out of the window into the garden. "You and Dad have got the garden looking nice. Mum would be pleased to see it looking so grand."

I put my arm on his shoulder. "She taught us so much."

Gramps always maintained his composure when talking about Mum. I could feel tears pricking, but tears of pride and happiness.

"She would be so proud of you," Gramps starts. He turns to look at me. "She was always so proud of you."

Stop now, Gramps.

He seemed to sense I was feeling wobbly.

"So, Dad was telling me about his new friend."

"Sarah?" I ask.

"Yes, how's that going? He shouldn't feel as though he can't date again."

"I think he just hasn't found the right person yet, but he has seen Sarah a couple of times now so it may develop," I tell him as I switch the kettle on. I'm obviously wary of just what to say about Jamie at this point. Should I tell him that

Sarah is Jamie's mum? I'd love to tell him all about Jamie. I'm sure he would be totally fine. But not today. Today was Gramps' Day.

Well, who knows?" Gramps says as he arranges cups on the tray. Everyone seems to just muck in here, which is great.

I take a long look out of the window. I'm so happy that Jamie gets on so well with Jordan and Katie, but who wouldn't? They are great friends. I stare at Jamie a moment. He is laughing at something Jordan said and looks relaxed. I don't think they know Gramps has arrived yet.

"Kettle's boiling, Danny." Gramps nudges my arm.

"Right, miles away for a moment," I say. I pour water into the pot and Gramps catches my eye.

Then, here it comes.

The question.

What vibes am I giving off?

"And, how about you, Danny?" Gramps ruffles my hair and has a twinkle in his eye.

"Me?" I stammer. "Oh, you know, too busy and all that. You know."

"Oh." He looks crestfallen and pulls a sad face.

What is he doing?

Then the twinkle is back again and he leans in. "I thought I was maybe going to get to meet your boyfriend today?" He looks across the garden to where the kids are sat.

Like. What. Just. Happened?

What?

Who did—?

What did he just ask?

"Gramps?" I question.

"Am I wrong?" he asks. "I apologise wholeheartedly if I am."

How did he know?

Has Dad been talking?

"Has Dad said something?" I ask tentatively.

"He didn't need to."

"Really?"

Gramps nods. "Really. So, Jamie is the one?"

I smile at him.

"Thought so." He gives me a sideways hug. "Do I get to meet him then? He's too far away to know if he's handsome."

I blush. "Gramps, what are you on?"

"There's not enough love in the world."

"What about George and Avril, do you want to meet him, well, like properly later, you know?"

"Oh, we've been talking about you and Jamie on the way here." Gramps waves dismissively. "They'll be just grand."

Do I have to say this again?

Like. What. Just. Happened?

These ageing folk know all about my love life.

Gramps just guessed?

Seriously?

Like, why? How?

I faffed about moving things around, checking the lid of the pot was on straight.

Gramps took my hand. "Come on, let's leave your dad in charge here. I need to meet the boy who has stolen my grandson's heart."

I can't believe this is happening.

Is everyone going to be so amazing about me and Jamie?

Shit. I'm not even sure how Jamie is going to take this.

Cripes, even Jordan and Katie might freak out.

Gramps pulls me outside and as soon as Katie sees him, she is on her feet and running. He is Gramps to everyone.

"Gramps!" she yells. "How long have you been here?" She throws her arms around him and gives him the biggest of hugs. Jordan is just behind her and Jamie is bringing up the rear. A bit more reserved but he has never met him, after all.

Gramps looks at me. "You said Jordan was coming?" He looks at Jordan and gives a crafty chuckle. "So, who's the lucky lady?"

"It's M&S Girl." Katie laughs.

"M&S Girl?" Gramps asks. "She must be pretty special if you've done all this for her." He waves his hand up and down in front of Jordan.

"She is, Gramps," I say.

All of a sudden, I'm nervous.

How do I introduce Jamie? Gramps mentioned the B word. Maybe I just go for it.

Jamie is stood sort of between Katie and Jordan now and I reach out and take his hand.

Even Katie is dumbstruck.

I pull him forward.

"Gramps, this is my boyfriend, Jamie."

There, it is done.

Gramps gives out a laugh and pulls Jamie in. "Special people get hugs, Jamie, and you are obviously very special in

Danny's life."

Jamie gives out a large gulp. "Thanks, Gramps. It's so good to meet you finally. Is it alright to call you Gramps? Sorry, everyone sort of said…" He trails off.

"I'll be very disappointed if you don't call me Gramps. Eh, Jordan?" He looks across. "Katie, has somebody stolen your tongue? You're extremely quiet, which is very unlike you."

Katie is still processing what has just been said. Jordan can't face even trying to think about it.

"I'm just," she starts, "well, did Jamie just get introduced as your boyfriend?" She looks across at me.

"Did I get it wrong then?" Gramps asks but in a joking way and with the famous twinkle in his eye.

Everyone looks at me as if they are frightened to answer.

I look round at everyone too. "No, Gramps, you didn't get it wrong, but I want to know how you knew if you didn't talk to Dad."

"You don't remember how you have been for the last few weeks? The things you've said about Jamie? You've been walking on air. You've had this stupid grin on your face. I knew something was up. You just confirmed it when we were making the tea. You were off in your own little world staring at Jamie."

"I swear, I don't know how you do it," I said.

"Are you both happy?" he asks.

Before I can speak Jamie comes straight in with, "I couldn't be happier, Gramps."

"Young love is just the best thing in the world and when two people are in love, it doesn't matter a jot about anything else." He looks around at us all then turns to face the house. "Now, we are going to be in big bother if I keep you all to myself. I know Avril wants to meet you all."

Katie tugs Gramps' arm. "Should we be quiet about Jamie and Danny?" she asks.

"No reason," Gramps says. "They both know." And with that, he heads off.

Katie looked at me. "What just happened?"

"I have no flipping idea," I say.

"Seriously?" Jamie asks. "I'm your boyfriend now?"

"Weren't you always?" I ask tenderly.

"Hope so." He puts his arm around me.

"Wonder how easy it would be to find some new friends who talked about boring stuff," Jordan says then laughs. "I got me the best friends in the world and no-one but no-one is taking you lot away from me."

We sort of group hug.

Couldn't have turned out better.

But I think Dad is looking a bit weird.

Gramps introduces everyone to Avril and George. I know it's his party but what the actual? "And this is Jamie, Danny's boyfriend," he says.

"You were right then," says George.

Dad looks at me and I just raise my shoulders.

"They make a lovely couple." Avril is hugging everyone. "Don't they, George?"

"They do." He laughs.

"Would someone tell me what is going on exactly?" Dad looks at each of us, not really taking in what is happening. "You didn't say you were telling Gramps."

"I didn't," I say, alarmed. "Don't blame me. I thought you

must have told him."

"Jack said something was afoot," Avril confides, "last time we saw him. He was full of it."

Dad and I exchange glances. I feel my life is being taken over by pensioners, but in a good way. Avril is lapping it all up.

"So, this isn't really my party but the day belongs to Jamie and Danny." Gramps is loving this. I wish Mum could have been here, the best day ever.

"No way." I shake my head. "This is your party, Gramps, and I for one need cake!"

Later

"What an amazing day." Jamie lies back with his head on my chest. We are alone in the summerhouse briefly while Katie and Jordan replenish the drinks. The olds have retired to the house, saying it's getting a bit chilly outside.

"Yeah, not bad," I say, stroking my hand over his head.

"I love your Gramps. He is so cool and amazing and wonderful and young. How on earth did he think I was gay? Why would it even cross his mind?"

"Who knows? But it's so cool that everyone is cool about us," I tell him, rubbing his soon-to-be-curly head.

"I guess it makes life a lot easier."

"I just think we are so lucky. Could have been so different." I love this boy. Did I tell you that?

We go quiet, enjoying being alone for five minutes.

"You did say gin and tonic, didn't you?" Jordan proffers me a glass, which has dark liquid in it.

"I didn't, no, but this is very definitely not gin anyway," I say.

"Oh, right, why did I say gin?" He flops down.

Jamie laughs. "Your friends are, well, different!"

Katie looks at Jamie and I. "You two look so cute."

I pull a face and Jamie burps after taking a large swig of Pepsi.

"Charming," she says "Cross that out and replace it with gross!"

Do we look cute? I feel so relaxed and very natural surrounded by the people who matter. Well, the people who matter and Avril and George. Who on earth are these people, really? I tighten my grip across Jamie's chest and he snuggles in.

Dad pops his head round the door. "Avril and George are leaving now. Do you want to come and say bye?"

We all jump up to say our goodbyes.

Avril gives everyone a hug and George shakes everyone's hands. Again. They are actually a lovely couple and have certainly taken to me and Jamie. He is top dog in their eyes and they chat amiably on the step. I'm sure they know all the history, you know, Mum and stuff, and just want us to be happy.

"Now, we insist that you come and visit us with Gramps sometime," George says. "We have had the most wonderful day."

"We will," we chorus. I'm not sure exactly who the invitation is for – I guess it is meant for Jamie and I – but Jordan and Katie will feel mega left out if we don't take them along too.

I gaze up at the clock. Where has the time gone? It's turned 8pm. Jordan catches me looking and whispers to me, "I should really be going. I've still got some homework to do for tomorrow."

Katie obviously hears him because Jordan and whispering don't go hand in hand, and she agrees she must be going too.

"How about you?" I ask Jamie. "You want to stay on a bit?"

"I would love to, but like Jordan I left some economics stuff, which I should attack. Would you hate it if I left?"

"Yes," I grumble but he can tell I'm joking. Or am I?

"You need to spend some quality time, just you, with Gramps. I hear he is staying over tonight."

"He is, yes," I agree, and it would be nice. Just me, Dad, and Gramps.

Jamie takes his phone out to contact his mum, to see if she would come and pick him up. Sunday buses are non-existent around these parts.

"Charlie, why don't you run these lovely people to their homes? It will save mums and dads coming out."

"Sure, guys," Dad says. "Gather your bits and I'll see you all home. The least I can do after all your help making today a perfect day."

I get a few moments with Jamie before he disappears off with the gang in Dad's car.

"Thanks for coming today," I say, looking into his eyes.

"You couldn't have kept me away," Jamie replies, running a finger down the side of my face. "I've had the most amazing day with a great bunch of people, but mostly, I got to spend time with you."

Bobby flutters for one last time in this story.

I reach forward and kiss Jamie passionately on the lips and he responds eagerly.

"Maybe next time, it will be just you and me." He smiles –

a mischievous grin and a sparkle in his eyes.

"That would be mega!" I tell him and hug him tight.

Three pairs of eyes are watching from the car. I glance over his shoulder.

"We have an audience," I tell him.

"Let's give them something for their money then." Jamie smiles and we kiss one last time before he runs off.

In moments the house is empty apart from Gramps and I.

"Well, young fellow, have you had a good time today?" he asks.

"I know I have. What about you?"

"It's been the best birthday ever." His eyes moisten. "Just a few other people it would have been nice to have here."

I knew who he means. Mum and Gran. Dad and I had thought the same, too, a few times today.

Gramps goes to sit on the couch and is looking thoughtful.

"OK?" I ask, sitting by him.

"I am," he starts. "I feel I want to tell you something."

"OK." I look into his eyes. He looks troubled. Shit, he's not going to tell me he's ill. Please, not that.

As if he read my mind, he grabs my hand. "I'm fine, Danny, nothing to worry about on that score."

"Phew," I say. I didn't want a lovely day spoiled.

"You know, things are so different for you young people nowadays." He pauses and looks off into space as if not quite sure how to continue. "You can express your love for Jamie so openly and you've seen the reaction you both got today, even from us old folk, which is lovely and just how it should be.

You and Jamie are no different to any young couple starting out."

He is quiet for a while and I don't interrupt, just let him take his time with what he wants to tell me. Maybe this is it; he just wants to tell me how lucky we are, and I certainly do feel lucky.

"Even thirty years ago you couldn't have legally walked down the street hand in hand." He pauses again. "Which is ridiculous." His voice is raised slightly. Why is he so angry?

Then he tells me.

"You know, my first love was a boy called Harry."

My breath catches.

"We were your age."

"You don't have to tell me, Gramps if..." I start, but then I'm unsure how to continue.

He shakes his head. "No, it's time I told someone. No-one else knows."

I have so many questions but feel it's inappropriate, so I sit quietly and listen while Gramps' tale unfolds.

"He had the most gorgeous blue eyes. Striking, you would say." He smiles at the memory. He looks me in the eye. "I think that's what attracted me to him. He was really kind, too. I was having, well, a bit of trouble in school and he stuck up for me. Some people called him a rogue, but he most certainly wasn't. He would walk home with me when he saw the troublemakers waiting by the gate. He didn't have to, but he did. Nothing was ever said. A lot of the time we just walked home in silence."

The floodgates were open now and Gramps needed to tell me his story.

"I don't know what I really felt. I think initially it was just safety. I didn't know what he felt either. I was always quiet at school and I think he saw that." Gramps looks at me again. "I wasn't even thinking about him in a, well, in that sort of way. I wouldn't even know how to think things like that. In the late 1960s it was all flower power but not same sex. You could still be put in prison if you were caught." His smile fades as he seems to remember something. "Then one day he asks if I'd like to go fishing, and I thought, no-one ever asked me if I'd like to go fishing, so I jump at the chance. We went down by the big bend in the river where the water is a bit deeper and slower moving. We ended up larking about a bit, but I was in heaven. Here was someone who was taking notice of me and I didn't really understand why. He encouraged me into the water; it was a warm day so we had taken off our socks and shoes and we cast our lines in. I ended up thinking I could go across to the other side, not knowing the river shelved off quite deeply and I ended up sliding in up to my neck." He laughs at the memory. "I can laugh now, but the breath was whipped out of me and I thought I was going to drown as my head went under the water. The next thing I knew, Harry had his arms under mine and was pulling me out of the water. He looked down at me. I was still a bit shocked but I looked up at him as he knelt over me and I said, 'You saved my life.' I remember it to this day. 'You saved my life.'

"And, he said, 'Do I get a kiss for it then?' And he leant in, and he kissed me, gently on the lips. There could have been anyone watching, but there wasn't, and I thought, blimey O'Reilly, is this what it feels like to kiss a boy?"

We both laugh, because I can remember having the exact same thought when I first kissed Jamie.

"Anyway, I stared up into those big, blue, sparkly eyes and was lost in the moment." He is pensive again for a few moments but I let him continue. "Then I thought to myself,

'Don't be stupid. Boys don't fall in love with each other.' I'd never even considered such a thing. I didn't know any man who was in love with another, but of course if they were, they just kept themselves very private, because like I say, it was still illegal."

I want to ask if there was more than one kiss but it doesn't feel right.

Gramps is quiet again for a bit, and then when he starts talking I feel he has jumped to the end of the story. Something is missing but maybe that's how he wants it to be. Leave me wondering, which is no bad thing.

"Like everything," he starts, "something comes along to destroy happiness."

I didn't want to know the bad part; obviously there was something otherwise I wouldn't have been here.

"Stupid Harry tells someone he had been kissing a boy, then this someone tells his dad and Harry disappears. To this day I'm not entirely sure where he was sent but Margate was mentioned, where he had two aunts who ran a boarding house. Lots of talk about the town of who this other boy was, and he should be ashamed, and if he was ever found out, well, as you can imagine I hardly slept for weeks, expecting a policeman to come knocking at the door."

"Oh, Gramps, that is so sad. What a time you had."

"So, of course I never even looked at another boy, although if I close my eyes I can still see those blue eyes. Life went on. Every boy met a girl and got married, and I'm not saying for one moment I didn't love your grandma. I worshipped the ground she walked on and I never ever talked of Harry to anyone."

"Do you ever wonder about him?"

"Sometimes. Back then I knew I couldn't do anything

about it and once I met your grandma, and your mum came along, I knew I didn't want to do anything about it."

I wondered how that must have felt. If Jamie suddenly disappeared, how would I react? Well, I knew the answer to that. Only a few short days ago I thought he had gone back home and I was distraught.

I realise had Gramps been born nowadays, his life could have been so different. He could have been me.

Then, flash, a lightbulb moment. I look him straight in the face. "So, is that how you knew?"

"Eh?"

"About me and Jamie? You knew because of Harry?"

"Oh, yes. I saw me in you. You hadn't even mentioned you and Jamie, but I knew the way you were talking and then the way you looked at him, it was like fifty-four years ago. It nearly felt like Harry was back."

"Wow," is all I could think to say.

"Indeed," Gramps replies quietly.

"I don't know what else to say. Your life could have been so different."

"It could, yes, but as I say, I've enjoyed my life. I've never hankered after going to find Harry or even any boy, and as you know, I've been on my own now for nearly forty years. I had the chance if I wanted to."

"You still have if you wanted to," I say, looking serious. "Not that you would, but then why wouldn't you?"

"No, I have my lovely memories and I have you and Dad, and not forgetting crazy Jordan, scary Katie, and the gorgeous Jamie." He chuckles, the spark is back in his eye.

I feel the story is over; he has said what he wanted to.

"Is this our story?" I ask quietly.

He looks a little puzzled.

"Just me and you know about Harry?"

"Oh, right, well, do you think I should tell your dad?"

"That's your call, Gramps." I can see a worried look. "I'd like it to just be us that know. I don't even want to tell Jamie. This is a special story of love between two boys and maybe Jamie and I can live out your hopes from back then."

Gramps squeezes my hand and I realise now he has held it all the way through the story.

Did it take courage for him to tell me?

Did he see himself and Harry in me and Jamie, but in a different era?

I so wish he had been able to see through his love for Harry.

Why had life been so hard for two boys back then?

I couldn't help but wonder if Harry had been strong enough to find another boy, maybe when he was older. Maybe they were running a guesthouse in Margate?

The front door opens and Dad shouts, "I'm back!"

I kiss Gramps on the cheek and whisper, "Thanks, Gramps. Love you."